SECRET OF THE GARGOYLES

GARGOYLE GUARDIAN CHRONICLES BOOK 3

REBECCA CHASTAIN

M
Y
M

Copyright © 2016 by Rebecca Chastain
Excerpt from *A Fistful of Evil* copyright © by Rebecca Chastain
Cover design by Yocla Designs

www.rebeccachastain.com

Mind Your Muse Books
PO Box 374
Rocklin, CA 95677

ISBN: 978-0-9992385-3-0

ALSO BY REBECCA CHASTAIN

THE MADISON FOX ADVENTURES

A Fistful of Evil

A Fistful of Fire

A Fistful of Flirtation

A Fistful of Frost

Madison Fox Novella Box Set

NEVER MISS ANY NOVEL NEWS: Join Rebecca's newsletter today!

Visit RebeccaChastain.com

For everyone who has made a wrong choice for the right reason.

ACKNOWLEDGMENTS

A trilogy! I'm still shocked that readers liked *Magic of the Gargoyles* enough to warrant expanding it into a series. Thank you, thank you, thank you! This book was by far my favorite—to visualize and to write.

Without my beta readers, this novel would have been published without the epilogue, and the ending would have been so much less fulfilling for the lack. For this advice and so much more, I'm grateful to have such wonderful people in my corner. Thank you, Cathy, Christina, Karl, Kimberly, Maghon, Rebecca, and Scott!

Thank you to my stellar editing team, Carrie and Amanda! Carrie, you're everything I could want in a copyeditor, and I appreciate the extra input you provide in your edits—including not letting me get away with superfluous phrases. Amanda, you've saved me from sounding like an idiot too many times to count, and I'm indebted to you!

Cody, I cherish your love, support, good counsel, and Photoshop skills. Thank you for backing my dreams!

Constructive Elements

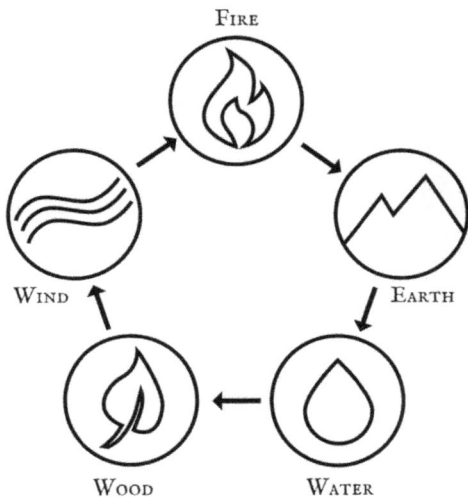

Fire

Wind

Earth

Wood

Water

Destructive Elements

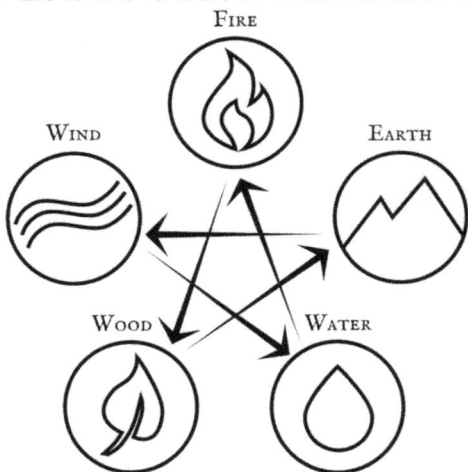

Fire

Wind

Earth

Wood

Water

1

fanned a tiny hummingbird feather back and forth, collecting the swirling air element from the breeze before scooping up the soft bands of fire element from a guttering candle flame. An equal mix of water element came from a bowl of spring water, and wood element from a pot of wheatgrass. Splitting my concentration, I kept the four-element cocktail spinning to one side and plucked a quartz seed crystal from my pocket.

I tuned a tendril of earth magic to quartz and used it to flatten and stretch the marble-size crystal. When the tensile structure of the quartz began to give, threatening to crack, I eased my magic out of the crystal. The flattened disk lay across my right palm, barely a foot and a half across and so thin it bent toward the ground around the edges. Hopefully it'd be enough.

"Stand back, Oliver," I said, glancing toward my gargoyle companion.

He undulated sideways, his carnelian Chinese dragon body moving as fluidly as a flesh-and-blood dragon's.

"Is this good, Mika?" he asked, studying the motionless sick gargoyle in front of me. Oliver didn't voice the doubts I read in his glowing sunset-orange eyes, and his magic boost never wavered. He wanted this to work as badly as I did.

"Yep. Here it goes."

The sick gargoyle's marmot body had once been a beautiful brown jasper, with vivid blue dumortierite tipping his reindeer antlers and long wings, but now he was pockmarked and only a few dull shades more colorful than gray. From his lifeless brown eyes to his rigid posture, everything about the marmot gargoyle looked dead, but he was only dormant. Inside him, a spark of life remained, and I was determined to wake him from his comatose state.

Ignoring the chilly morning air that brushed my stomach when I raised my arms, I lifted the sheet of quartz high above the gargoyle. Standing on his hind legs, the marmot was almost eye level with me, and his antlers cleared my head by several feet. Ideally, I would have placed the thin quartz across his antlers, but their points were too far apart, so I settled for positioning the quartz above his head. With exaggerated care, I layered the four-element mix across the surface of the quartz disk, gradually sinking it into the thin membrane until the clear crystal swirled with magic. Hardly breathing, I collected air to cushion the bottom of the quartz, then retracted my hand. The disk remained floating above the marmot.

Crossing my fingers, I backed up, buried my eyes in the crook of my elbow, and dropped the quartz onto the marmot. The fragile sheet shattered, tiny grains spraying against my thighs. I lowered my arm. The five elements rolled down the marmot, coating his crown and ears, then muzzle, neck, wings, and stomach before sliding off his bottom toes and the tips of his stone feathers. The moment it touched the ground, the spell dissipated.

A fine glitter of quartz dust circled the marmot, and it crunched under my feet when I stepped closer to examine him. The gargoyle's eyes remained dull. His ears didn't twitch. Weaving a basic five-element pentagram, I tuned it to the gargoyle's resonance and tested him. His life pulsed against my magic, the reedy sensation encased in muted pain.

"No change." I brushed quartz dust from the marmot's upraised paws, then blew more from his forehead with a heavy sigh. It'd been silly to get my hopes up.

Many people believed gargoyles went through a dormant phase as a normal part of their lives, opting to check out for decades at a time, but my healer instincts said otherwise, and one test of the marmot's failing health had backed up my suspicion. Gargoyles typically enjoyed a sedentary life, choosing to remain near specific buildings for most of their days, but they still moved. Frequently. They were also picky about whose magic they enhanced, yet this paralyzed marmot gave a magic boost to anyone in the vicinity, as if his powers were as out of his control as his limbs. He was trapped inside his own body—and he wasn't the only one. I'd found six other dormant gargoyles in Terra Haven stuck in an identical dormant state.

"What now?" Oliver asked.

"We try something else," I said, which was better than saying, *I don't know*.

I slumped, dropping my forehead to rest against the marmot's. I'd already tried everything I could think of. I'd attempted healing him with and without Oliver's enhance-ment, beneath new and full moons and all the days in between, using exotic, expensive resources and basic seed crystals. I was running out of ideas—even the desperate ones, like today's modified, outdated spell originally designed to heal lethargy in humans—and the marmot was running out of time. Never strong to begin with, his life signs grew fainter every day. Even the other dormant gargoyles fared better than he did, but not by much.

Familiar weariness pulled my eyes closed. In the three months since I'd first learned about the comatose gargoyles, I'd been searching for a cure nonstop, and sleepless nights bent over my table scouring increasingly obscure references combined with a series of hope-crushing failures had sapped my energy.

"We'll find something, Mika." Oliver planted a paw on my hip, nuzzling my side, and I staggered beneath his weight.

"I know. Together we can do anything." The words tasted bitter.

A shouted curse pulled my head up, reminding me we weren't alone in Focal Park. A few hundred feet away, one of the cleanup crew tumbled into an enormous sinkhole, only to swing back up to solid ground on thick bands of air wielded by her four coworkers. She clutched the arm of the woman who grabbed her while one of the men reinforced the crumbling cliff, using hefty bands of earth element to reshape the granite beneath the topsoil and strengthen their footing.

The eroded crater in the middle of Terra Haven's premier park hadn't occurred naturally. Neither had the mutations in the botanical gardens or the flow of now-cool magma that had decimated a fifth of the grounds. The entire park had been deformed, all thanks to Elsa Lansing.

May she rot in prison.

Elsa had attempted to manually re-create a gargoyle's magical enhancement in an inanimate invention and failed spectacularly, nearly destroying the city along with Focal Park. But that was the least of her sins.

I ran a finger over five smooth patches on the marmot's neck. The clear crystal integrated into his fading brown jasper neck was my healer handiwork, and it'd taken me over a month to coax his weak body to graft enough layers of quartz to seal the five stab wounds. It turned out that to mimic a gargoyle's enhancement, Elsa had required the magic of a gargoyle, and she'd had no compunction against drilling into the marmot and draining his life to fuel her invention. Comatose and paralyzed, the marmot hadn't been able to fight back or even flee.

Rotting in prison was too good for Elsa, and knowing her invention had nullified her, leaving her unable to ever touch the elements again, was only a small consolation.

The earth rumbled behind me where towers of three-foot-wide granite pillars jutted from what had been a smooth slope before Elsa's invention went haywire. One of the taller granite posts snapped off at the base, then flew across the park to hover above the sunken ground. Cables of wood element pulverized the rock, crumbling the entire thousand-pound column into the gaping earth. Magic glowed around all five workers, funneling through the woman who had fallen into the pit, as they selected another pillar to demolish.

If not for my status as Terra Haven's sole gargoyle healer, I would have been banned from the hazardous park with the rest of the city's citizens during the restoration process. Instead, I had special clearance to tend to the marmot and one other dormant gargoyle in the park. The other, a large fox, lay out of the way atop a high granite outcrop, but after righting her internal imbalance caused by the invention's malicious magic, I'd stuck to the more accessible marmot for my healing experiments. He'd had the good sense to be on level ground when sickness struck, not perched at a vertigo-inducing height.

"Let's get this cleaned up, then see if the library has received the journal we special ordered," I said, unable to infuse any enthusiasm into my words.

"She's here," Oliver whispered.

My shoulders stiffened. I didn't need to turn to know he meant the onyx and amethyst gryphon gargoyle. She'd been following me around for the last month, observing from a distance any time I interacted with a dormant gargoyle—a critical witness to my repeated failures.

The first time she'd shown up, I'd thought she'd come to help. Every gargoyle I'd asked about the dormancy sickness refused to talk to me about it except for Oliver and his four siblings, and they were as perplexed as I was—by the disease and by the other gargoyles' silence. But the gryphon was different. She'd helped me in the past: When Oliver had been a baby, he and his siblings had been kidnapped and imprisoned by Walter, a mercenary earth elemental who had tortured them to steal their magic for himself—and for the highest bidders in his black market scheme. While I'd been desperately trying to rescue the hatchlings, the gryphon had convinced the city guards to investigate my wild tale. Without her timely arrival, I wouldn't be alive, and neither would Oliver or his siblings.

I'd been wrong about her intentions now, though. The gryphon refused to let me or Oliver get close enough to talk, and I'd grown to resent her judgmental presence. It was bad enough that I hadn't found a cure after months of research and experimentation; having an audience made it ten times worse.

I ground my teeth and used a soft push of air to sweep the quartz powder into a pile. With Oliver's help, I packed up my supplies, the weight of the gryphon's censure boring into my back the entire time. Irritation made my movements clumsy. I didn't need the gryphon to point out my deplorable incompetence; I lived it every day, watching the dormant gargoyles slowly fade while I tried useless spells. My frustration with today's failure was made worse by the fact that I'd never really expected the spell to work; I simply hadn't had anything better to try—and I hadn't for weeks. But the gryphon's silent condemnation was the final straw.

"I've had enough of this." I spun and locked gazes with the gryphon. She lurked closer than normal, and I could easily make out her glowing lavender eyes, despite her location in the dappled shadows fifty yards away.

"Do you need help?" I called, my tone conveying the *butt out* meaning of my words. I projected my voice through a cone of air to direct it toward the gryphon and away from the cleanup crew. I didn't need them sticking their noses into this, too.

The gryphon's neck feathers ruffled, and sunlight ghosted across the ripple of onyx. Her hard eyes remained expressionless.

"Look, I'm doing my best here." I shrugged off Oliver's placating gesture and stomped up the incline toward the gryphon. "I'm trying everything I can think of, so unless you have any suggestions—"

The gryphon surged forward, leaping into the air on stone eagle wings and hurtling straight for me. I dropped to all fours to avoid being clipped by her massive eagle talons, my heart lifting into my throat. The backdraft of her wings whipped my hair into my eyes as she shot past us. She banked, spinning through the air as if she'd anchored one wingtip in the ether, and swooped back toward us. Her enormous body temporarily blocked the sun before she landed on silent stone feet close enough to snap my head off. Oliver reared up protectively in front of me, but even with his wings flared, his slender body looked fragile next to the gryphon. She ignored him, folding her enormous amethyst-striated onyx wings against her body and glaring at me.

"Stop shouting." The gryphon's voice was that of a lion's, soft and rumbling, despite forming in a rock throat and emerging through an eagle's beak.

"Uh, of course." I straightened on shaky legs and squared my shoulders.

Dismissing me and Oliver, she stalked around us to stare into the marmot's blank eyes. I released a quiet breath and patted Oliver. He dropped to all fours, keeping his wings partially cupped to give himself extra bulk. I shuffled in a wide arc around the gryphon until I could see her face again, and Oliver twined beside me, moving slower than normal. I think it was his version of being tough, and I appreciated the effort.

"I've been watching you," she said.

"I know—"

She turned the full weight of her stare on me, and my mouth clicked shut.

"I have talked with the gargoyles you've healed," she continued, "and I have talked with the gargoyles this cub has been spreading tales to."

Oliver bristled, the orange-red ruff around his face flaring. I crossed my arms. Was this where she accused me of being an unfit healer? If so, she was wrong. I'd been an exemplary healer—at least until I'd encountered the comatose gargoyles. She was welcome to point me in the direction of a more practiced healer or even a book that might provide an answer to the dormancy sickness, but otherwise I wasn't in the mood to listen to her recriminations.

"You risked much to save the hatchlings when they were so foolishly caught. You risked more to save Rourke."

My indignation faltered. She knew the sick gargoyle's name.

"I'm still trying to save him—to save Rourke," I said. "But you know that. You've watched me every day."

The gryphon acted as if I hadn't spoken, observing without speaking as the cleanup crew broke off another pillar of granite, spun it through the air, and crumbled it into the deep pit on the other side of the park.

I tried to read her expression. She didn't look ready to chase me out of town for being a miserable healer. She looked more torn than angry.

Had I misjudged her? Was it possible she wasn't here to berate me? Something had made her approach me today, and I bit my lip to hold in a babble of questions and demands that might scare her off.

"You have proven yourself twice, Healer, and perhaps you've even earned the honorific this pup has been claiming. It's been centuries since we've known a true guardian."

I twitched as if she'd poked me. Oliver had started calling me *guardian* after I'd saved the marmot and a half dozen other gargoyles Elsa's invention had ensnared while it'd been tearing up the park. I hadn't put much stock in it. He was young and worshipful, and working with *Guardian Mika* sounded more impressive than *Healer Mika*. I hadn't realized the title meant anything, but the gryphon implied it did.

"If I'm going to trust you . . ." She pivoted on a hind foot and paced away from me and back, tail lashing. "If I'm going to save you . . ." She paused to peer into Rourke's faded eyes. With a choked roar, she spun away and thrust her beak so close to Oliver's snout that their breaths mingled. My brave companion didn't flinch.

The gryphon's voice rumbled with anguish when she asked, "Is she really a guardian? Is she worthy?"

"My life is hers," Oliver said.

"You are too young to know what you say."

Oliver quivered, wings flaring in anger. "I've held her spirit inside me. My age doesn't matter. I felt her in my heart. I know Mika is a guardian."

I shuddered at the reminder. I'd once transplanted pieces of my spirit into Oliver and his four siblings in a colossally stupid maneuver that would have shredded my brain if it hadn't worked. At the time, it'd been the only option I could use to save the gargoyles from being ripped apart by Elsa's invention, and I hadn't fully considered the ramifications. Nor had I realized Oliver had been able to glean anything from that piece of me, let alone that it was what convinced him I was a guardian.

I was beginning to suspect the title of *guardian* was more than an honorific, too.

The gryphon broke off her staring match with Oliver and straightened to turn her piercing regard upon me. I did my best not to fidget, but my bubbling hope made it difficult. If I guessed correctly, she knew what could save the marmot—what could save all the dormant gargoyles—and she seemed to be talking herself into telling me. I hunted for the right words to convince her I deserved her trust, but the longer I looked into her glowing amethyst eyes, the more certain I became that nothing I could say would be enough. Either she believed me worthy or she didn't.

I crossed my fingers behind my back.

"Guardian." The gryphon paused as if testing the word. "My name is Celeste, and I place the lives of all gargoyles into your hands with what I am about to tell you."

2

Celeste scanned the park and I found myself checking our surroundings, too. The cleanup crew was too far away to hear and no other creatures were close. Nevertheless, when she spoke again, it was barely above a whisper, the rumble of her words mixing with the cracks and groans of pulverized granite.

"Rourke's cynosure baetyl was gravely injured."

Oliver reared back, every spike and feather on his body standing on end as he shook his head. I glanced between him and the hunched gryphon, alarm quickening my pulse.

"His what?" Baetyls were stones believed to be of divine origin, but what did that have to do with gargoyles, and how did a rock serve as a guide?

"That's not possible. Nothing can harm a . . . a baetyl." Oliver barely mouthed the last word and his wide eyes darted in every direction.

"What is a cynosure baetyl?" I hissed.

"Home," Oliver whispered with a shiver. "We shouldn't talk about it."

"A baetyl is where we hatch," Celeste said.

"On a stone?" I pictured a rock nest high atop a mountain where tiny baby gargoyles were born and took their first flight.

"Inside, not on. Baetyls are underground. They're sacred, secret places without which no hatchling would survive. We need our baetyl's magic to be born, and we need it again throughout our lives to rejuvenate our bodies."

"We do?" Oliver asked.

Celeste lowered herself until she lay on the ground to get closer to the young gargoyle's eye level. "It is a compulsion you'll feel when you're older. Your body knows when it needs to return. You're far too young to have experienced it, but if you are too long away from your cynosure baetyl, you will eventually weaken and become unbalanced."

I crouched to hear her whispered words. Baetyls hadn't been hinted at in any book or journal I'd read. For centuries, scholars and healers had speculated on the birthing rituals of gargoyles, but the few who had broached the subject with gargoyles had been rebuffed. I understood their need for secrecy. If unscrupulous people like Walter and Elsa knew where they could find weak gargoyles and helpless newborns, the gargoyles would never be safe.

"Wait! Walter! Did he defile your baetyl, Oliver?" The man still lived, imprisoned, but if even a chance existed that he could get his hands on more baby gargoyles . . .

Oliver shook his head. "No. We were outside the . . . outside home when he captured us."

I relaxed my white-knuckle grip on his shoulder with a sigh of relief. Celeste watched us with unblinking eyes, waiting until we'd focused on her again before continuing.

"Rourke is over a half century overdue to return to his baetyl. The only reason he's survived this long is because of his location."

"What do you mean?"

"He was not the first of his baetyl to sicken. We watched others fade into comas, and some died fast. Some didn't. Survival depended on seclusion; those in public places fared better and lived longer. We hunted out the location with the most concentrated number of humans actively using magic. The park used to be that place before it was destroyed."

"That's why he boosts everyone in the area," I said, the answer to the mystery clicking into place. Gargoyles fed off the magic they enhanced. It was why they gravitated toward busy public buildings and the homes of powerful full-spectrum families. Full spectrums could wield all the elements with a strength I could only come close to with quartz, and when a gargoyle enhanced someone that powerful, they fed off a wealth of magic. By passively enhancing everyone who came close enough, Rourke and the other dormant gargoyles had been able to continue to feed even as their bodies shut down. I'd been afraid I had missed some dormant gargoyles hidden in less populated areas, but she just confirmed I hadn't. Sadly, any who had fallen comatose somewhere out of the way would already be dead.

Celeste's eyes tracked the cleanup crew as she spoke. "Even if they finish fixing the park tomorrow, I fear that if Rourke goes much longer without contact with his baetyl, he'll die. So many have already wasted away. I may have doomed us all, but I cannot abandon my mate to that horrid death."

"Rourke is your mate?"

Celeste nodded.

"And he's been like this"—I gestured to the frozen gargoyle trapped in his own body—"for over fifty years?"

"He and all the rest from his baetyl. There used to be

twenty-three. There's no one left to speak for them, none to judge you for themselves, so I am acting on their behalf."

My heart broke for Celeste. She'd watched her mate's life wither away for decades, unable to do anything to help him without risking the lives of every gargoyle.

"Thank you for trusting me, Celeste. I'll make sure he and the others get home to their baetyl." It couldn't be that simple, could it?

Celeste shook her head as if answering my unspoken question. "They tried to go back years ago. Rourke said his baetyl had been injured and he came back sicker than before. I took him to my baetyl, but it pained him too much to stay."

"A baetyl can't be injured," Oliver said, his voice small and uncertain. He'd huddled into a tight bundle, and for the first time in months, I thought my six-foot-long companion looked little.

"Anything can be hurt, even baetyls," Celeste said.

I finally realized what she was asking of me. "You don't need me to heal Rourke. You need me to fix the baetyl."

"It is my last hope."

Relief washed the strength from my limbs and I sat. I had an answer to the dormancy sickness. *I had a cure.* I even understood why Celeste had taken so long to come forward. In telling me about the existence of baetyls, she'd endangered the lives of all gargoyles. Even Oliver had never mentioned a baetyl to me, and he trusted me with his life. For all Celeste knew, I could publish the information, and then there'd be a mob of unscrupulous scavengers hunting for baetyls and the helpless gargoyles inside. She'd had to extend her trust even further in asking me to fix Rourke's baetyl: To fix it, I'd have to be told its exact location.

I have a cure. I repeated the words again in my head to

savor them. This morning I'd despaired of finding a remedy in time, and now . . . *I have a cure.* The words reknit my confidence. My inability to cure the comatose gargoyles hadn't been my fault. I'd been attacking the symptom, and the problem wasn't even a part of the gargoyles. It existed elsewhere, outside their bodies.

The ramifications of that thought dampened my satisfaction. The problem existed *outside* the gargoyles.

"When Rourke said his baetyl was injured, did he mean the baetyl itself or the baetyl's magic?" I asked.

"They're the same thing. A baetyl's magic is the baetyl," Celeste said, confused by my distinction.

"Is a baetyl's magic like a gargoyle's?" I was a quartz savant, but my skills with normal five-element magic weren't half as impressive. It meant I could perform amazing feats with quartz-tuned earth, which was how I became a healer of gargoyles and their living-quartz bodies, but the rest of my abilities were midlevel at best.

"A baetyl's magic is . . ." Celeste hunted for the right word.

"Everything," Oliver said.

Celeste nodded, as if he'd made sense.

I tamped down my frustration, knowing they weren't being purposely obtuse. We were close to saving the dormant gargoyles. All I had to do was figure out how to fix a baetyl, which as far as I could tell was either a cave with magic or a form of magic contained in a cave.

A magic that could heal comatose gargoyles. A magic that was *everything*.

Fixing a cave I could probably do, especially with the help of gargoyles to boost my magic. Fixing a form of magic itself sounded beyond my capabilities.

"How big is a baetyl?" I asked.

"I've never been inside Rourke's, but probably no larger than this park," Celeste said.

I struggled to keep my expression blank. Focal Park covered over a square mile. I was hopelessly out of my depth.

"Are you asking me only because you don't think you can trust anyone else? I can find you others—" *Stronger elementals.*

"No. No one else has a chance of helping," Celeste said. "You're the closest thing to a gargoyle who can work magic. If any human can integrate with the baetyl's magic, it is you, Guardian."

Oliver nodded in agreement.

I stared at them both in astonishment. They saw me as a pseudo-gargoyle? It was flattering and perplexing all at once.

"You're sure this is the only answer? Maybe I could replicate a baetyl's magic here," I suggested.

"You couldn't even come close. This is the only way."

Of course it was. "Once I fix the baetyl, Rourke and the others will recover?"

"After they've spent long enough inside it, yes."

I took a deep breath and modified my previous plan to include finding the secret location of Rourke's baetyl, carting over three thousand pounds of frozen gargoyles inside, and *then* repairing a form of magic I knew nothing about in a cave larger than several city blocks. Because I was a guardian or because I was the equivalent of a human gargoyle, Celeste believed me capable of all three impossible tasks.

I'd have to be, too, since seven lives depended on it.

"You don't happen to know where his baetyl is, do you?" I asked.

"Of course."

My spirits lifted. "Really? Where?"

"Waupecony Ridge."

Her words punched my gut and I deflated. "You mean Reaper's Ridge?"

3

The Native Americans hadn't been poetic when they named the white quartz–laden peak Waupecony Ridge, or White Bone Ridge. They understood the perils of the mountain, but early settlers wouldn't listen to their warnings, especially not once they saw the veins of gold lacing the snowy quartz. From the beginning, there were reports of Waupecony Ridge miners who lost their memory and even more who wandered from the mining camps only to be found days or weeks later, starved, dead, and often the snack of local predators.

Then the Hidden Cache Mining Company had purchased rights to the entire ridge and begun large-scale mining. They pulled a fortune from the mountain for several years—right up until forty-three of their miners were torn asunder in a freak explosion of wild fire and earth magic. It was the first in a battery of elemental storms, and when they couldn't be contained, the federal government had decreed the area too dangerous for continued operation. That hadn't prevented the elemental storms raging across the hillsides from claiming a life or two a year, killing hikers and fortune hunters too foolish to heed the restrictions, earning the area the nickname Reaper's Ridge.

Occasionally, a Federal Pentagon Defense squad would be dispatched to Reaper's Ridge to subdue wayward storms, and even the elite FPD warriors couldn't do much more than enforce a wide perimeter around the ridge.

Why did the baetyl have to be there?

"I can't do this on my own. I'm going to need help," I said.

"I'll help," Celeste said, and Oliver seconded her.

I nodded, not really listening. I would have preferred going to Kylie for assistance. She was my best friend and had helped me in the past, but she was out of town, covering the blooming of the everlasting tree for the *Terra Haven Chronicle*. Even if she were available, she was a journalist at heart. Dangling exclusive information about gargoyle birthing grounds in her face, then telling her she had to keep it a secret, would be pure torture. More practically, she didn't have the physical strength, magical know-how, or warrior training I'd need to survive Reaper's Ridge. I needed the help of seasoned full-spectrum elementals. I needed Captain Grant Monaghan and his squad.

When I said as much to Celeste, she leapt to her feet and loomed over me. "You can't tell anyone, especially not *five* more people."

Despite her menacing stance, she didn't scare me this time. I knew her posturing was born of fear, not a desire to hurt me. Nevertheless, I stood up, walking to Rourke's side to put some space between myself and the incensed gryphon.

"You said you don't know how much more time Rourke has. We need to work quickly, and I trust Captain Monaghan and his squad with my life. He was the one who led the efforts to save Rourke and the park." He'd done more than that: It'd been Grant and his team of FPD warriors who had saved the city, and they'd trusted me to work alongside them to help injured gargoyles. If anyone could get us through the storms on Reaper's Ridge, it was Grant's team.

Grant also happened to be the only leader of an FPD squad that I was on a first-name basis with and the only one who would believe me if I said my perilous mission was necessary. More important, he and his squad were the only people I would trust with this secretive mission.

"They are not guardians. They cannot help," Celeste insisted.

"I wouldn't suggest we go to Grant's squad unless I thought they were necessary *and* trustworthy," I said. "Think about it. How would I get Rourke to the baetyl by myself? I can't carry him, and even if I could, what about the others? How would I protect them from the wild storms? As much as I'd love to do this on my own, I need help. This isn't a one-woman mission."

Lacking the muscles to carry a gargoyle didn't bother me, but admitting to being too weak as an elemental to protect them rankled. The gargoyles of Terra Haven depended on me. If I couldn't be everything the gargoyles needed, then it was up to me to make sure I found others who could shore up my shortcomings.

It took an hour of circular arguments before I convinced Celeste, and when she finally agreed, she insisted we leave immediately. I concurred; we didn't have any time to waste.

We exited the park together, with Oliver and I staying well clear of Celeste's snapping tail. In the early days after the destruction of Focal Park, Oliver and I had drawn a lot of attention. Few gargoyles left their rooftop perches and fewer still walked the streets with a human companion. With Kylie's front-page "Gargoyle Healer Saves Terra Haven" article fresh in everyone's mind, complete with a picture of Oliver and me, we couldn't have been more recognizable if we'd carried signs. But after a few weeks, the small crowds we'd drawn in our wake had faded. We'd become neighborhood fixtures and recipients of friendly waves and greetings, which I much preferred.

With Celeste stalking at my side, we were back to spectacle status. I ignored the stares and pointing fingers and concentrated on what I'd say to convince Captain Monaghan to help us.

Every few blocks, a fresh wellspring of gargoyle-enhanced magic burst open inside me. The unexpected gush of available magic repeatedly caught me off guard, tripping me mentally and physically even though I should have been used to it by now. Ever since the incident in Focal Park, gargoyles had started providing magic boosts for me whenever I was in range, whether or not I was using the elements at the time. Since gargoyles were particular about who they enhanced and typically didn't attempt to boost an elemental who wasn't actively using magic, it was flattering. Oliver claimed it was a sign of respect for a guardian, but up until today, I'd dismissed his explanation as a by-product of his hero worship. I couldn't help but notice that with Celeste accompanying us, the frequency of the boosts had increased threefold, as if her presence added weight to my reputation.

I acknowledged the offerings with waves and nods to the serious gargoyles who watched us pass from their high perches, for the first time in a long time feeling worthy of their favor. I had a real plan to help the comatose gargoyles, not just desperate hopes and ineffective remedies. Thinking about Reaper's Ridge, I amended the thought: I had a plan *and* desperate hopes.

Oliver was the only one of us who'd ever been to the squad's home base, so he led the way. None of us spoke as we left behind the bustle of downtown and climbed the gentle hills on the east side of Terra Haven. Enormous mansions jutted along the tops of the rolling crests, but we turned onto a flagstone pathway halfway up a slope and stopped in front of a bright yellow two-story stucco house with a nine-foot-tall wooden door. Celeste flew up to the roof, landing soundlessly on the terra-cotta tiles and disappearing. I steeled myself and knocked.

No one answered. I waited a minute, counting the seconds as they passed, then tried again, pounding the iron knocker against the wood with all my strength. Eleven seconds later, the door burst open and Marcus Velasquez loomed over me. I fell back a step, then caught myself. Cold blue eyes burned into me, and a muscle bunched in his anvil of a jaw. Recognition dawned a second later, and the rugged fire elemental's intimidating pose relaxed fractionally, but his forbidding expression didn't alter. Without saying anything, he crossed his tan arms—a move that emphasized his thick biceps and wide shoulders—and leaned against one side of the door frame, obviously waiting for me to speak.

A flurry of bubbles rioted in my stomach.

"I . . . Is Grant here?" I squeaked.

Sometime during the catastrophe at Focal Park, I'd developed a crush on Marcus. The last time I'd seen him, I'd even convinced myself that he was interested in me, too. But I'd been too busy hunting for a cure for the dormant gargoyles to devise a casual way to bump into him and reassess my feelings for him under more normal circumstances—like when he wasn't saving my life—and he'd never sought me out. After a few months, I decided I'd made everything up, my crush included.

Up until five seconds ago, I'd believed myself, too.

"Hi to you, too, Mika Stillwater." His deep voice rolled through me.

"Hi, uh, Marcus." I flushed. *Get over yourself. You're not here to ask him out. You're here to help Rourke and the other gargoyles.*

"Hi, Marcus," Oliver said.

"Hey, Oliver." The gargoyle got a small smile.

"Is Grant here?" I managed to get the words out without sounding strangled this time. Bully for me.

Those cool blue eyes fastened on me again, and I wondered what had ever made me think he might have been interested in me. It'd clearly all been a euphoric side effect of my near-death experiences. Marcus was an accomplished fire elemental in an FPD squad. He was so far out of my league he may as well have been on another continent.

"He's out."

"Seradon?" I asked. The squad's earth elemental had liked me. She'd help.

"Out."

"Winnigan?" My voice came out too high.

Marcus's lips twitched and he finally took pity on me. "Everyone's on vacation. I only stuck around because . . ." His eyes scanned over me and he exhaled with a rueful chuckle. "Because I'm an idiot waiting for something that's never going to happen. Come on in."

Before I could protest, he turned and padded barefoot back into the house. Oliver loped over the threshold and across the tile floor, and his puzzled glance over his shoulder prodded me into motion. I stepped into the house Marcus shared with the squad and shut the door behind me, hurrying to catch up with Oliver. We trailed the fire elemental across a wide room filled with couches and tabletop games and through open French doors into a sun-drenched courtyard. Marcus settled into a cushioned bench, stretching one leg along the entire length. Oliver hopped onto the wide rim of a fire pit and curled his body around the cool coals. I stood awkwardly at the edge of the courtyard.

"How long until they're back?"

"One, maybe two weeks."

"Two weeks!" Celeste dove into the courtyard, blocking out the sun with her enormous dark wings.

Marcus rolled off the back of the bench, sprang to the wall, and spun back with a slender sword in one hand, a ball of fire in the other. My heart lurched into my throat, and I leapt forward, shoving through wicker furniture the large gargoyle had carelessly scattered, but by the time I'd forced my way between Marcus and Celeste, he'd extinguished the fireball and the sword hung loose at his side.

"Anyone else I should know about?" Marcus asked, his tone casual but his body still tense.

"We can't wait that long," Celeste said, ignoring him.

"I know. Is Grant close?" I asked. "Can we reach him? Maybe an air message? What about the others?"

"He's not in Terra Haven. He went to see the everlasting tree bloom, and the others decided to tag along."

Of course they had. I'd be there myself if I hadn't been busy with the dormant gargoyles. It wasn't surprising that the captain just happened to be in the same place as Kylie, either.

Marcus narrowed his eyes at me and stalked back into the sunlight. "You clearly didn't drop by to tell me you've missed me. What have you gotten yourself into, Healer?"

"It's better this way. No one else needs to know," Celeste said.

"We can't do this alone. We already agreed—"

"Fine." She examined Marcus from head to toe. "One person is better at keeping a secret than five."

"But to fix the . . . the *thing*, I need more than just his help. I was counting on being linked with five full spectrums." Linking meant I'd be able to draw on the combined strength of all five powerful elementals. With all their magic plus a boost from Celeste and Oliver, I had a chance of fixing a baetyl the size of the park. With just Marcus, our odds of success plummeted.

"Mika . . ." Marcus growled.

"You won't need to link," Celeste said.

"How can you be sure?"

Celeste shrugged. "A link wouldn't do you any good. You're a guardian. They aren't. They probably won't be allowed inside."

My throat constricted, and I forced myself to take a deep breath. Celeste's assurances did nothing to ease my trepidation, but I'd already agreed to do everything in my power to help Rourke and the others. Maybe she was right and I wouldn't need the might of five FPD warriors backing me. Maybe one would suffice.

But before I could fix the baetyl, we had to get there.

"Are you sure we can't contact Grant?"

"Tell me what's wrong," Marcus said.

I met his steely gaze. Experience had taught me that Marcus was calm under pressure and highly skilled. If I suppressed the embarrassment of my crush, we'd work well together; we'd done so in the past. Plus, one full spectrum was better than none.

"I know how to heal the dormant gargoyles, but it's

complicated and requires something outside Terra Haven. I need help," I blurted out. "And if you agree to help us, I need your sworn oath that you will never reveal anything I tell you. Not even to Grant."

Marcus's expression closed down, and as he studied me, he twisted his wrist, swishing the sword back and forth around his leg.

"Please," I added when the silence became unbearable.

He stalked to the wall and returned the sword to its hiding spot in the rafters. When he came back, he sat on the bench, legs stretched in front of him and crossed at the ankles. "Tell me."

"Swear first, human," Celeste said.

Marcus arched an eyebrow at her. "I swear."

I accepted a boost from Oliver and formed a soundproof bubble of air to wrap around the four of us. Marcus crossed his arms but didn't say anything.

"Do you know about cynosure baetyls?" I asked.

He shook his head, and despite his superior knowledge of the world and magical creatures, I wasn't surprised. The gargoyles had guarded this secret with their lives.

In a few short sentences, I summed up everything I knew about baetyls for Marcus, finishing with, "It's been decades too long for all of them. If the dormant gargoyles don't get to their baetyl—their repaired baetyl—they'll die."

"Why have I never heard about baetyls before?" Marcus asked.

"You shouldn't know about them now," Celeste growled, her lashing tail slowly pulverizing a wicker chair. Marcus didn't seem to notice.

"Celeste only told me because I am a guardian." I stumbled over the title.

"I take it that's different than a healer."

"Vastly," Celeste said.

"How?"

"That's like asking what the difference is between fire and a fire elemental," she said, and Oliver nodded sharply.

Obviously Marcus had never heard of a gargoyle guardian, if he had to ask. Judging by his grunt, I didn't think he was impressed.

"What's the catch?" he asked.

"The broken baetyl is on Reaper's Ridge."

"No." Marcus stood, forcing me to tilt my head back to maintain eye contact.

"So you won't help me?" I hadn't expected him to leap for joy, but I hadn't expected him to refuse, either.

"No, I'm telling you *you're* not going."

"You...you're *telling* me," I sputtered. Planting my hands on my hips, I curled my fingers into the fabric of my shirt to control my rising temper. "I'm not asking for permission."

"That's not permission; that's advice. If you go, you'll die."

I leaned forward, matching him scowl for scowl. "Wrong. I only *might* die." Okay, that had sounded better in my head. I plowed on. "But if I don't go, all seven of the dormant gargoyles *will* die. I can't stand by and let that happen, not when I can save them."

"When you *might* save them. There's no guarantee. Do you even know how to fix a baetyl?"

A year ago, I hadn't known how to heal a gargoyle, and now I was a gargoyle healer. If Celeste thought I could fix a baetyl, then I'd figure it out. But I was smart enough not to say as much to Marcus. Fortunately, he didn't wait for a response.

"FPD squads have attempted to tame Reaper's Ridge multiple times and have paid for it with their lives. Those were hardened groups of linked full-spectrum elementals. What makes you think you could survive five minutes?"

He wasn't telling me anything I didn't know, but I'd been doing a stellar job of burying my dread by focusing on the cure. Now all my fear clambered to the surface. I could tell he saw it in my eyes, and it pissed me off.

"Why do you think I'm here? I know I need help. You know what, though? This was stupid. Forget I said anything. While you're at it, forget I ever told you about baetyls."

"Mika—"

"No. I'll do it without you."

I spun toward the exit but Marcus stepped into my path before I made it two steps. I had the option of running into him or stopping. If I'd thought I stood a chance at moving him, I might have considered ramming him. Instead, I settled on the best glare I had and aimed it at his throat.

"You don't understand." I tried to sound calm, but I only managed to sound like I was holding back tears. "I don't have a choice. That's where the baetyl is; that's where I have to go. I can't let the gargoyles die, not without trying."

His pulse bounced in his throat and his Adam's apple bobbed when he swallowed.

"Move. Please. I have a lot to do."

Oliver whined, jumping down to stand beside me. Celeste loomed in my periphery.

"You're really going, even alone, aren't you?"

"Yes."

"We'll be there," Oliver said.

I glanced at Marcus's face. The man could tunnel through a brick wall with that scowl.

"This is the most idiotic idea I've ever heard."

"No one asked your opinion."

Marcus snorted. "Fine. I'm in."

"You're coming?"

"Someone with brains needs to be on this venture."

I swayed in place with the intensity of my relief. I wouldn't be doing this alone. I'd have preferred the whole squad, but Marcus's abilities were nothing to scoff at. Maybe, just maybe, we'd survive.

"When do we leave?" he asked.

"Today," Celeste said.

"Then we've got a lot of work to do."

We were really going to Reaper's Ridge. I swallowed against the urge to vomit.

4

I strained to hold my bands of air under the seated sardonyx tiger. Even boosted as I was by Oliver and Celeste, I wouldn't have been able to lift the large statue-like gargoyle much more than a foot off the ground by myself. She was one of the largest of the dormant gargoyles and outweighed me by at least five hundred pounds. It didn't help that I was already tired from moving the other six, first from their locations throughout the city and into the quarry cart Marcus had rented, then into the freight car. My magic quivered like an overworked muscle, loose and too flimsy for one more repetition.

Marcus swooped a thick basket of air under my strands and the swan-winged feline floated from the back of the cart and through the wide loading door of the freight car. Together we settled the gargoyle onto the wooden floor-boards, maneuvering her between a warthog-headed bear and Rourke. Once I determined she was stable, I released the elements and collapsed against the side of the metal car, swiping sweat from my forehead.

Seven lifeless-looking gargoyles filled the floor of the freight car, leaving enough room at the front for two canvas-lined cots and little else. The gargoyles' frozen forms had made squeezing them into the tight space a bit like assembling a puzzle—one where the lightest piece weighed over a hundred pounds.

Marcus had impressed me with how quickly he'd mobilized everything. In the time it'd taken me to rush home and pack, he'd hired a quarry cart and driver; then we'd spent the last few hours riding around Terra Haven, collecting the dormant gargoyles. Somehow, he'd also booked us a private freight car on the last train out of the city, and we'd finished loading the gargoyles with a few minutes to spare. It would have taken me an entire day to collect the gargoyles on my own, even if I could have lifted them by myself, and I didn't know the first thing about renting freight cars. I started to thank him, but he dismissed me with a flat look and turned to pay the cart driver. Marcus had been helpful but about as pleasant as a bee-stung bear. He hadn't complained once or attempted to talk me out of the trip after he'd agreed to go, but his attitude made his opinion about our quest perfectly clear.

I did my best to ignore him and focus on being grateful for his help. Standing in Emerald Station helped.

Eight tracks and four loading platforms fanned across the station, all protected by an arching canopy of vines. Honeysuckle and wisteria blossoms scented the air, mingling with the baser smells of grease, metal, and sweat. People milled around the open shop fronts of the station or lounged among the wooden seats, and a talented fire elemental wove elaborate scenes of pure flame as he told stories to enraptured children. Too many people were in the way for me to get a good view of his show as I caught my breath, but I saw a few spectacular birds made of fire.

I hadn't been on a train since a middle-school field trip, when we'd embarked on an exciting overnight stay at a sister school a city away. I'd lived for months in anticipation of the adventure. The same bubbly excitement stirred in my stomach now, mixed with anxiety and fear. This wasn't a fun excursion to another city; we were headed straight into forbidden territory, and the lives of these seven gargoyles depended on me not only surviving but also somehow restoring a place I'd never seen to specifications known only to comatose gargoyles.

A heavy rumble and clanging pierced by the shrill whistle of steam brakes announced the arrival of another train on the opposite platform. The bittersweet odor of burning grass and clouds of cooling steam billowed from the engine before the soft elementally enhanced evening breeze dissipated them. Up and down the train, coach attendants opened passenger doors with timed precision and identical flourishes, and men and women poured out. Grabbing bags, they jostled their way through the passengers hurrying up the platform to board our train.

I glanced up to where Oliver perched atop the freight car. He stood with his back arched and tail high, his carnelian orange-red body glowing in the lights of the massive hanging chandeliers. His head never stopped moving, taking in the busy scene below him. He had an adventurer's spirit, so unique in a gargoyle, and I was grateful every day that he chose to be my companion.

Situated at the prow of the freight car, Celeste stared straight down the tracks toward our destination. Where Oliver preened when he noticed people pointing at or admiring him, she appeared to have tuned out the world. As a rule, gargoyles didn't ride the trains. Why would they when they had wings to fly? The sight of two on a single freight car sent ripples of curiosity through the crowds.

Most people didn't look twice at the dormant gargoyles we'd loaded, though. To the casual observer, they could have been confused with statues, and if anyone noticed a moderate boost to their magical strength when they walked by, they probably attributed it to Oliver and Celeste.

I pushed away from the freight car and brushed the front of my pants, dusting off a layer of dirt. The heavy staccato bangs of a gong growing closer pulled my head up. The conductor swaggered through the crowd holding the line to the train's khalkotauroi, a massive bull too tall to see over with heavy bronze feet and a bronze muzzle. He followed the slender woman docilely, chewing his cud, and when he exhaled a belch of fire, the conductor caught the flames in a ball of water element and reduced it to a hiss of steam.

All without taking her eyes from Marcus.

"I'd heard some jerk made a last-minute addition to my train," she said, her husky voice cutting through the cacophony of conversations around us. "I should have known it was you, Velasquez."

Marcus turned, his face lighting up with The Smile. Ruggedly attractive when he wasn't trying, when he smiled *that* smile, he transformed into breathtakingly handsome. I'd been the recipient of The Smile a time or two. It was powerful enough to knock my thoughts sideways. The conductor merely quirked an eyebrow.

"You better not delay our departure," she said. Her chin-length black hair swung into her face when she stopped, and she tucked it behind her ear. Standing between the khalkotauroi and Marcus, she looked fragile and elfin, but her sultry dark eyes swept over Marcus as if she were sizing him up for dinner.

"Naomi, when have you ever known me to slow things down?"

A sour flavor coated my tongue, accompanied by the visceral churn of jealousy in my gut: They were flirting. Ugh.

I grabbed the edge of the open freight car door and hoisted myself inside. Lacking coordination after the long day, I tripped on the tiger's tail and stumbled into Rourke, hugging him to regain my balance.

"Is she okay?" Naomi asked.

"She's fine, just a little slow in the head," Marcus said.

I glared at him over my shoulder, but he and Naomi missed it, both too busy looking into each other's eyes.

Face flaming, I gave Rourke a pat and twisted through the rest of the gargoyles to my cot at the front of the car, only then sneaking a peek out the open door again. The beautiful conductor radiated confidence, which wasn't surprising; she had to be a strong fire elemental to do her job. Plus, she and Marcus had *history*. It was there in her body language when she casually touched his arm and echoed in his relaxed posture. And The Smile. The one that reappeared with nauseating frequency. Here was a woman in Marcus's social stratum. Viewing my crush alongside Naomi made it all the more pathetic.

I growled at myself, imitating the noise I'd heard most frequently from Marcus today. It didn't matter what the man thought of me. It mattered how helpful he was with saving the gargoyles.

Pushing the squirmy ugliness of jealousy down, I reached for my bag. I'd stowed it earlier under my cot, and I had to stand back up to get the leverage to budge it now. Underneath my change of clothes and snacks rested forty pounds of a gargoyle healer's best tool: seed crystals. Pure quartz and infinitely malleable, the seed crystals could be used to heal all manner of physical injuries, including being grafted onto a gargoyle to replace chipped or severed body parts.

Four fit comfortably in my hand and I rolled a few more into my pockets. Then I walked among the gargoyles, checking them with gentle probes of magic. Their life forces flickered with the same muted strength as they had before we'd carted them from their resting places, with little variation between each gargoyle. The years had been equally cruel to them all, pockmarking their skin and eroding rough patches. I could feel the peripheral ache of these wounds when I delved into each gargoyle, but I didn't know how much awareness the dormant gargoyles possessed.

For Rourke's sake, I hoped it wasn't much.

I don't normally have violent feelings, but I'd entertained a lot of fantasies in the last months of stabbing Elsa so she could see how it felt. She'd viewed Rourke as nothing more than a tool to be used. She hadn't seen him as a living creature, and she hadn't cared about hurting him. With people like her in the world, it was no wonder gargoyles were more willing to let the dormant ones die rather than risk exposing their vulnerabilities to humans.

"I'll never tell," I whispered to Rourke. "You're safe with us."

"Oliver, Celeste, do you want to come inside?" Marcus asked, swinging up into the freight car. Behind him, the massive khalkotauroi plodded toward the engine, his copper hoofbeats reverberating through the station. A cart piled high with hay bales trundled behind him, pulled by a pair of station stable boys. The giant fire-breathing bull would need a lot of fuel to power a train this size through the mountains.

"I'm going to stay up here," Oliver said, hanging over the edge. His tongue lolled from his mouth, his grin looking twice as goofy upside down.

"Come down through the front if you change your mind," Marcus said, pointing toward the human-size door at the front of the freight car.

Celeste didn't answer. She'd been quiet all day after we'd convinced Marcus to help. I didn't know if she was naturally recalcitrant or if her worry kept her silent.

The train released three shrill whistles, and coach attendants repeated the signal with their smaller silver whistles. A few more people rushed by the open door, racing to board before we pulled out of the station.

Marcus tossed two balls of fire into the brass lanterns, using quick flicks of air to close the glass shields around the lit wicks, and then swung the enormous loading door shut. It rumbled on its runners and closed with a deafening clang of metal on metal, locking me inside the windowless container with seven mostly dead gargoyles and one grumpy fire elemental.

————

I SPENT THE FIRST HALF HOUR ON THE TRAIN SITTING STIFF and self-conscious on my cot, pretending to read a novel about a courtesan spy. Or maybe about a princess con artist. I couldn't keep the story line straight, but I kept turning the pages and trying to look natural. I'd fretted over getting the gargoyles to their baetyl and surviving Reaper's Ridge. I'd pictured all types of caves buried in the mountain and had run through dozens of techniques I'd used on gargoyles, hoping one of them would suffice for the baetyl. But I'd failed to consider the actual night spent on the train. Alone. With Marcus.

He'd lain down on his cot after we'd pulled out of the station and we'd checked to ensure the rocking motion of the train wouldn't topple any gargoyles. He hadn't opened his eyes since. I didn't think he was asleep, but I couldn't be sure.

With the rhythmic *clack-clack* of the tracks beneath us and the gentle sway of the freight car, it was hard to maintain the level of urgency that had hounded me in Terra Haven. Without that sense of dire purpose, the terrors of Reaper's Ridge filled my thoughts.

The storms that tore it apart were composed of raw, wild magic, completely unpredictable and impossible to control. If we got trapped inside a storm of pure fire element, we'd be burned alive in seconds, and it would be the most merciful way to die. I'd heard the horror stories of the bodies found—from drowning victims lodged in trees to frozen remains discovered in the middle of the summer. There'd even been a few instances of people who had seemed to explode, as if the wild magic had burst them apart.

Snapping my book shut—which elicited nothing, not even a twitch, from Marcus—I bounced to my feet and yanked open the door at the front of the car. A rush of roasted grass–scented air swirled into the freight car and lifted my hair from my neck. I stepped out onto the small platform and shut the door behind me. Two steps took me to the iron railing, and I leaned out to put my face in the wind.

Terra Haven had disappeared behind gently rolling hills covered with yellowing grass and dotted with trees.

Through gaps in the hills, I spotted the glint of Lincoln River and the lush fields of crops along the banks, but our route took us northeast around the mountains, and the river wouldn't be in sight much longer.

I pushed away from the railing and hopped the slender gap between cars, then opened the door to the overnight car in front of our freight car. When I closed the door, my footsteps slowed in the hushed atmosphere. Most of the right side of the car was walled off into a dozen smaller quarters for privacy and sleeping, and the empty walkway was weighted with silence. The faint aroma of lavender and thyme lifted from the thick carpet with each of my steps, and I lingered by the tall windows on the left to watch the hills roll past before the growl of my stomach urged me on.

When I opened the door to the passenger car, a dozen faces turned to stare at me before dropping back to their papers and books. I patted the overhead railing to keep my balance in the rocking car as I walked up the length, and I did my best not to touch anything else. The car was immaculate. Plush red velvet seats with small brass buttons and armrest accents were set in groups of four around marble-topped tables complete with place mats folded into fans, crystal goblets, and real silverware. Most of the car's occupants were dressed fine enough for a temple ceremony, not in dusty jeans and a T-shirt like I was. Even the black and gold carpet was swept clean, and when I passed him, the coach attendant tsked and used a soft brush of air and earth to erase my footprints. I mumbled an apology and rushed through the door.

I crossed the gap between cars again and pulled open the next door, relieved to find the dining car. I made use of the washing fountain in the corner, which had its own attendant who cycled the water and cleaned it with a complex weave of air, water, earth, and wood to remove the grime I'd added to the basin.

A galley kitchen ran along one wall and dining tables along the other. A group of women decked out in leather flight gear and colorful tunic tops lingered over drinks at a table set against the window, talking animatedly about the differences between flying dragons and pegasi, but otherwise the car was empty. I purchased two roasted vegetable potpies, which were made fresh for me while I watched, and half a loaf of rosemary sourdough bread. The chef presented the meal on a silver tray, the potpies in porcelain bowls, and the spoons were silver and wrapped in cloth napkins. He added a saucer with several pats of butter, two teacups, a fan of tea bags for me to select from, and a pot of boiling water. Staggering under the unexpected bounty, I wove carefully back to our freight car, exerting the full strength of my air ability to keep everything on the platter and upright when I navigated between cars.

When I stepped into the freight car and closed the door behind me, Marcus cracked an eye.

"Are you hungry?" I asked. It seemed like a rhetorical question since we hadn't stopped for food all afternoon, and Marcus must have agreed. He sat up and silently helped me with the platter. We didn't have a table, so we set it on the floor between us and braced it between our bags so it wouldn't slide when the train leaned around a curve.

"We're attached to a first-class train," I said.

Marcus grunted and reached for the bread, tearing it in half.

"You got a freight car attached to a first-class train," I repeated.

First-class trains were the fastest on the line and given top priority, which meant all other trains were shunted to the neighboring track or were held at a station to keep the track clear for this train. Used almost exclusively by the wealthy, first-class trains didn't haul freight, and they didn't make stops at abandoned stations.

"You said it was urgent," Marcus said.

"It is, but I can't afford this." I could barely afford the dinner I'd bought us.

"The FPD is picking up the bill."

Really? That was news to me. "Thank you." I couldn't make my words flow together, and they came out in stilted phrases. "And for helping me. With the gargoyles. Even though it's going to be hard."

He watched me while he chewed, face unreadable. Finally he swallowed. "I said I would help."

"I know. And I hadn't thanked you. So ... thank you."

"I haven't done anything yet."

That sounded like the start of an argument I didn't want to have, so I looked away from his intense stare and took a bite of the potpie. The crust melted on my tongue, flaky and buttery, and the sauce of the cooked vegetables was so delicious that I stopped chewing to savor it. Swallowing a moan of delight, I forgot about Marcus and concentrated on enjoying the gourmet meal. Far too soon, I swept the final drops of sauce from my bowl with the last bite of bread. I stuffed the morsel into my mouth and leaned back, eyes closed, indulging in a moment of pure satiated bliss.

When I opened my eyes, Marcus's unreadable gaze lingered on me. Self-conscious, and reminding myself how out of my league Marcus was and how mortified I'd be if he ever found out I had a crush on him, I stood up and squeezed into the middle of the dormant gargoyles. I knelt beside the tigereye fox from the park. Hardly the size of a bear cub, she lay curled into a circle, all her feet and her nose hidden under her fluffy stone tail.

I gathered a soft mix of elements to test her health—

Something heavy slammed into the front door, denting it inward with an explosive thunderclap of sound.

5

Marcus launched to his feet, a coil of magic swirling against his hand as he shoved the door open.

Celeste stuck her head in, but her wide shoulders caught on the door frame, halting her forward momentum with a shriek of protesting metal. Cool evening wind whistled through the open door, blowing my hair into my eyes.

"Rourke needs magic! He's fading!" she yelled, grabbing the frame with her massive eagle feet and wrenching. The metal screamed but held.

"Calm down!" Marcus barked. His authoritative posture was ruined a moment later when Oliver catapulted from Celeste's back through the door above her head. Marcus ducked and threw himself against the wall with a curse. Oliver's slender body fit easily through the narrow doorway once he tucked his wings tight, which meant he plummeted like a rock to the floor, shattering our dinnerware. Immediately, he unfurled his wings and launched over the gargoyles straight for me.

I flung myself to the ground, covering my head with my hands. Oliver clipped the side of the freight car with a wing, deafening us all with the metallic reverberation. He landed heavily on the back of the black and white onyx wolf next to me, scrambling to maintain his perch on the gargoyle's slick fish-scale sides and smooth flying-fish wings. His long tail struck me in the shoulder, knocking me sideways, and I scrambled to a safer location under the large tiger.

"Mika! They need help!" Oliver shouted.

"Everyone, *CALM DOWN*!" Marcus bellowed. "Celeste, let go of the door. Oliver, get your snaky butt over here." He pointed to the empty floor space between our cots, kicking the dented silver platter out of the way and scooping the broken porcelain of our dishes into a net of air before tossing them out the open door. Oliver tried to take off, slipped, and crashed onto the fox. The impact shook the floor of the freight car and made my ears ring. Before I could check to make sure he was okay, he squirmed to his feet and wriggled to the location Marcus·indicated. I crawled out from under the tiger and checked the fox. Bits of her tail had flaked off and a dull pain radiated through her body, but it was the weakness of her life signs that alarmed me.

"What's the problem?" Marcus demanded.

"We're too far from the city. Damn it! I'm an idiot." Celeste had told me the only thing keeping these seven gargoyles alive had been their location in prominent, magic-laden places of Terra Haven. We'd removed them from the only thing sustaining them. I explained as much to Marcus even as I opened myself to the magic boost all the dormant gargoyles offered so they could feed off my magic. Compared to the magical enhancement of a normal, healthy gargoyle, their boosts were a mere trickle, but the amount of magic they offered wasn't important.

"We have to use magic for them," I said. "They need to feed on it. They've basically been starving for decades, surviving on the scraps they could consume indirectly from people who used them for magical boosts. If they don't get more magic, and quickly, they'll waste away."

I hooked my heavy bag with a band of air and tugged. It wiggled in place, but I couldn't lift it. Then fresh magic gushed into me, and I felt Oliver in the enhancement—his eager energy and the coil of excitement that never dimmed inside him. A moment later, even more magic poured into me from Celeste, but I wouldn't have been able to distinguish the signature of her enhancement the same way I could Oliver's. Months of working closely together had tuned me to him in a way I hadn't known was possible.

Filled with magic, I wove cables of air and levitated my forty-pound bag more effortlessly than if I'd lifted it with my hands. As soon as it was in reach, I removed a seed crystal and began reshaping it to patch the fox's wounds. Fortunately, they were minor enough that I could knit her tigereye flesh into the new quartz, closing a half dozen nicks without overtaxing her delicate system.

"What can I do?" Marcus asked.

"Use the elements—and use their boost to let them feed off you."

A few seconds later, the pummeling wind abated and the car quieted as Marcus coated the opening with a solid sheet of air, wrapping it around Celeste's head when she refused to back up. A glow of fire element swept through the freight car, countering the cold air with a gentle heat. I stepped among the dormant gargoyles, checking each of them. The flicker of their lives stabilized, but they were all frighteningly weak.

"We can't keep this up indefinitely," Marcus said.

"I don't think we'll have to. As long as we make sure they get regular doses of magic, they should be okay."

"How regular?"

"I don't know. I've never done this before." I wasn't even sure I was right, but I hoped I was. Neither of us could sustain a steady volley of magic from now until we reached the baetyl, not even Marcus and not even if we took turns.

Once I was sure no other dormant gargoyles had been injured, I squeezed through them to Oliver's side.

"I'm sorry. I got scared. I didn't mean to hurt her," he said, head drooping. "I wanted to help."

"It's okay. She's fine, but you're not." A ragged patch had chipped from the ruff around his square face like a bad haircut, and the orange carnelian wound was sandpaper rough.

"It's no big deal," he said, despite flinching away from my delicate touch.

"Nothing we can't fix in a few seconds," I agreed. "And you're always an incredible help."

Oliver didn't say anything, but his wings relaxed and he lost his hangdog expression.

I floated a seed crystal to my hand and reshaped it as I knit it into Oliver's injury. At one time, it would have taken all my concentration to mold the crystal and weave the complex elements to mesh the inert quartz with Oliver's living carnelian body. Now I could do it almost without looking.

"Can you feel how much stronger the others are already?" I asked when I finished.

"No."

"You can't?"

"He is not mated," Celeste said. She no longer looked ready to rip apart the freight car, so she must have been able to feel Rourke's increasing stabilization.

Marcus floated the abused silver platter in the air in front of him, rotating it over an intense blue-white cone of flame. While I patched Oliver, he reshaped the softened metal, removing the claw-foot dents Oliver had embossed in it. Then Marcus meticulously re-etched the swirling leaf design through the cooling silver until the platter looked better than when I'd taken it from the dining car.

He glanced my way, and I snapped my mouth shut. Of course Marcus could do the precise work of an artisan. Just because he looked like he was built to run through granite walls, had the elemental strength to match, and spent his time fighting the worst magical creatures and problems in the city didn't mean he couldn't do delicate work with his magic, too.

"How much longer do we need to keep this up?" he asked.

I looked to Celeste. The gryphon stared over my head at her mate, worry sitting strangely on her eagle face.

"Awhile longer," I finally said.

"Are you done there?" he asked.

"Yep. But we need to keep using magic." I gave Oliver a pat and he snuggled against my legs. The clear quartz I'd used to rebuild his chipped ruff to its previous shape looked peculiar among his orange-red rock fur, but in a few days, his body would absorb the crystal and replace it with carnelian.

"It doesn't matter what we do with the elements?"

I shook my head, hunting for ideas. I could blow wind around the freight car and maybe pull a few drops of moisture from the air, but neither would keep much magic moving for the dormant gargoyles to passively feed from.

"How about a game of Elemental's Apprentice?" Marcus asked.

"The kid's game?"

"Got a better idea?"

I sighed. "No."

Elemental's Apprentice was a game of humiliation. The premise was simple: Using only magic, two people tossed raw elements back and forth, sometimes with physical items included. The person who dropped the elements first lost. The easiest way to win was to toss your opponent more element than they could handle. Since I'd always been only a midlevel earth elemental with even weaker skills with air and water, I'd almost always lost, usually getting drenched with water in the process. Against a full spectrum, I didn't stand a chance.

"Let's start with air," Marcus said. He sat on his cot, his back to the wall with the broken door and his legs stretched out. Everything about his posture said he was relaxed and expected an easy victory.

"Sure." I shifted to sit cross-legged on the floor and Oliver curled around me, eyes glowing in anticipation. Pulling on my connection with the gargoyles, I collected a massive bundle of air, weaving the element into a tight vortex and plucking a few strands loose so it'd unravel the moment Marcus caught it. I wasn't going to make this easy on him.

"Whoa. Hang on," he said. "I didn't mean a battle to the death, and I see what you're doing there with that trap. It wouldn't work, but that's not the point. We just need to keep magic circulating, right? Let's keep this friendly."

I shifted the vortex to the side so I could study him. He looked sincere—and amused.

"For the gargoyles," he added.

Still not trusting him, I dispersed my wind-funnel trap

and made a small fist-size bundle of air, then wrapped and tied it off so it would hold its form once I threw it. I tossed it to Marcus and immediately prepared a wall of earth magic in front of me in case he hurled it back five times as big and too fast for me to catch. Instead, he lobbed it back, scoffing when I had to drop my barrier to catch it.

"Not a fan of the game?" he asked.

"I've played with a few poor sports."

"The kind who set traps in their first throw?"

I didn't appreciate the implication. "The kind who enjoy humiliating those weaker than them. You know, typical full-spectrum superiority crap." I threw the air back to him with more force than necessary.

Oliver tilted his head against my thigh as he tracked the air ball's flight back to me in the heavy silence. I rested a hand on his side and let out a long breath.

"Sorry, that was uncalled for," I said, reminding myself Marcus had never done anything but help me.

We threw the element back and forth a few times before Marcus asked, "Do you know a lot of full-spectrum elementals?"

"Personally? Just you. And Grant and the rest of the squad," I added quickly. "But as a kid, there were a few in my school. I wasn't sad when they got transferred." Some of my friends had been jealous of the more talented students and the special school they'd been whisked away to in their early teens. I'd been relieved to see them go.

"You're lucky. I know a lot of full-spectrum pricks."

My gaze snapped to Marcus's, and he winked.

"I was one of them for a while. I could teach you some dastardly tricks some other time. Beef up the air, then add water."

"Are you testing my control over the elements I'm weakest with?"

"Yes."

"Why?"

"Because tomorrow we're going to Reaper's Ridge, and I want to see what you've got."

I frowned. "You know what I've got. This isn't the first time we've worked together." Even if he'd forgotten when we'd fought together in Focal Park, we'd spent today linked. The intimate combining of our magic would have left Marcus with no questions about how weak I was in every element.

"Which is why I didn't agree to come with you just because you gave me puppy-dog eyes. I know you're not going to flip out, but you're handicapped by that whole everyone-else-first healer thing."

"What's that supposed to mean?" *Puppy-dog eyes?*

"Tomorrow will be about more than throwing yourself in front of every threatened gargoyle. You'll actually have to try to survive." His scowl was back in full force.

"That's the plan," I said, confused by the turn in his mood.

His mouth flattened. "Grab some water and let me judge if you're capable of two things at once."

"And here I thought it was just a friendly game." He'd seen me do far more complex divisions of magic than handling two elements at once. I'd hoped having a little food in his stomach would offset his sour mood, but it'd been too much to ask of a single meal, even one as spectacular as the potpies.

I wound together a bundle of water element strands and prepared to throw it to Marcus.

"No. With water."

"What water?" I asked, looking around. Oliver had smashed the teapot.

"Gather it up."

I examined the spray of moisture staining the floor, then Marcus. He raised a challenging eyebrow. Gritting my teeth, I got to work. Pulling the droplets together took more of my concentration than I would have liked. I fumbled the air ball, dropped it once, and had to shave it in half to keep it under control before I finally wrapped strands of water element around a collected handful of water, encased it in a bubble of air, and floated the wobbling blob off the floor.

"Bring it on," Marcus said, not commenting on my sloppy work.

I lobbed the water inside my thin barrier, hoping it'd break apart and drench him. Instead, Marcus caught it, combined it with a separate perfect sphere of water I hadn't noticed him collect, and tossed it back to me as I released the air ball toward him. I caught the water, wrapping it in thicker elemental bands to stabilize it.

In between throws, I sent tiny probes of magic into the dormant gargoyles, checking their health levels. They hadn't gained much strength, but they were no longer weakening. Celeste had relaxed, too, and the worry had eased from her expression. She'd curled up on the open threshold, but her head remained high and she watched Rourke like, well, an eagle.

"Why do you feel more comfortable with water than air?" Marcus asked, breaking the silence and startling me into almost dropping the air ball.

I'd half resolved not to speak to him again, but his tone had lost its bickering edge, so I responded. "My parents are both water elementals."

"Really?"

"Pretty strong, too. They spent a lot of time working with me to help me perfect my limited ability."

"Where'd you get your knack for earth?"

"I don't know. No one in the family had an affinity for quartz like I do."

"Add in some earth. No. Make it quartz. I should get some practice."

As easily as thinking, I'd collected earth element and tuned it to quartz. For reasons I'd never been able to explain, I was stronger with quartz than I was with untuned earth. I used to assume it was because I'd practiced with the element so much, but lately I'd been considering I might have been born with a specialized strength. Quartz had always been easier for me and more accessible. It was only as an adult that I'd thought to use it to make a living. Then I'd met Oliver and his siblings, and my life had been completely changed.

For the fun of it, I wrapped the quartz-tuned earth around three seed crystals, then tossed them to Marcus. He caught it and fumbled, the crystals clattering against each other like castanets, but recovered quickly. I took petty delight in his lack of perfection.

"Wood, too," he said.

I dutifully wove pure wood into a knot and bounced it to him. Marcus added a cotton rag from his bag to give the element weight. If not for the gargoyles' extra magic, I would have had a hard time holding all the separate elements together with air, but with their help, keeping four elemental balls alight wasn't even tough.

"Now fire," Marcus said.

I made a glowball. Marcus returned it with a two-inch flame fluttering at its heart. I caught it delicately, looping it back to the fire elemental from a safe distance. Schools forbade playing with real flames. Losing control of a bucket of water was messy but easy enough to clean; losing control of naked fire could cause permanent harm. That didn't mean I hadn't tried—and walked away with singed eyebrows.

"It won't bite," he said.

"I'm rather partial to my hair," I muttered.

Marcus chuckled. The warm light of the lanterns and the bouncing flame softened the hard planes of his face, and his mirth held a hint of The Smile. I pulled my gaze away before he caught me staring and focused on the arcs of elements between us.

For a while we let the muted *clack-clack* of the metal wheels across the seams of the rail fill the silence. Outside, the sky had darkened, and the scenery through the gap of the missing door had become lost in the shadows. Reaper's Ridge and all the dangers it presented were still a day away, and for the moment, no urgency pushed against my thoughts. In this warm environment so far removed from the real world, it seemed perfectly natural to strike up a conversation with Marcus. We skirted around discussing tomorrow and the dangers awaiting us, sticking to innocuous topics like our pasts—my rather ordinary upbringing in a known-for-nothing town, his adventurous military experiences and exciting missions with the FPD—our favorite places to eat in the city, and the best temple for the summer solstice.

While we talked, we tossed the elements back and forth until our moves were so synchronous I didn't have to think about them, which was probably Marcus's intent. The whole game was likely a strategic plan designed to familiarize me

with working with him and vice versa. I didn't care. I
enjoyed the moment of comfortable normalcy—something
I'd lacked during the frantic months I'd searched for a cure.
I also monitored the dormant gargoyles. When their life
signs had been stable for over an hour and Celeste had fully
relaxed, I reluctantly ended our game.

"You should get some sleep. You'll want to be rested for
whatever we face tomorrow," Marcus said, tossing the water
out the open door and resealing the air barrier. He let the
other elemental bundles dissipate, and the cotton cloth fluttered to his hand. I caught the seed crystals with a scoop of
air and dropped them into my bag.

Oliver had fallen asleep tight around me, and I had to
wake him to free myself from his stony embrace before
hobbling on stiff legs to my cot. Stretching out, I toed off my
boots and pulled the scratchy wool blanket over myself.
Marcus dimmed the lanterns and settled on his cot. The
cozy atmosphere morphed, turning the friendly energy into
something intimate and awkward as I listened to him
arrange his covers. Tension crept back into my muscles, and
I thought it would keep me awake, but the rocking of the
train lulled me to sleep minutes later.

———

I WOKE LOOKING INTO CELESTE'S GLOWING AMETHYST EYES.
Marcus breathed softly on his cot, asleep, and Oliver lay
stretched out and sleeping on the floor beside me. I couldn't
tell how long I'd been asleep, but I guessed it'd been a few
hours. Softly, I reached for the dormant gargoyles, testing
them. They'd weakened. Not as much as before, but I didn't
want to take any chances.

Rolling quietly to my feet, I tiptoed into the middle of

the gargoyles, where I'd left my bag of seed crystals. I sat and wriggled my chilled toes into my boots, then opened myself to the gargoyles' boost. After carefully heating the air in a weak version of Marcus's spell, I decided to do what I did best: work with quartz.

Before I'd become a gargoyle healer, I'd had ambitions of being Terra Haven's preeminent quartz artisan. Now that goal felt juvenile and shallow. Nothing compared to the joyful rush of healing a sick or injured gargoyle, and the most prestigious artistic accomplishment couldn't compete with saving a life. However, I still enjoyed creating beautiful objects with quartz and it kept my skills sharp, and the money I made selling quartz jewelry and figurines at a gallery in the city augmented my sporadic healer income.

Drawing as much as I could hold of all the elements to help feed the dormant gargoyles, I separated delicate strands of earth, fire, and air to combine several seeds into a blob. With practiced ease, I twisted the lump and stretched it into the most popular figurine I sold: a replica of Oliver. Normally I used carnelian to match his distinctive body, but the clear quartz did a good job of catching the light and refracting it through the small details of his eyes, ears, and folded wings.

As soon as I finished, I started the next figurine, making one for each of the dormant gargoyles, then a few of Celeste. I strung together ten crystals and created the train, complete with miniature people on the inside and the khalkotauroi in the engine car, clear hay strands scattered around his feet, clear flame breathing from his nostrils to heat the water. I left out Conductor Naomi.

Sleep weighted my eyelids, and after a while, I reclined on my side with my head propped on the curled fox. I planned to doze for only a few minutes, but when I woke, indigo sky was visible through the open door and the glow of the sun lit the edge of the horizon.

Today was the day—either I was a guardian, capable of fixing a baetyl and saving the comatose gargoyles, or I wasn't, and everyone in our party could die for my hubris. I prayed I wasn't handing Reaper's Ridge its next victims.

"Naomi agreed to let us use her private bathroom, but you'll need to be quick to make it through the train without disturbing the passengers," Marcus said when he noticed I was awake.

I grimaced, not needing the reminder of the gorgeous conductor before I'd fully woken; thinking of Reaper's Ridge had made me queasy enough already. But refusing the offer out of spite would cause only me to suffer. Besides, my bladder didn't care how Marcus had convinced Naomi to give us access to her quarters. I grabbed my bag and scurried through the open door. When I returned in fresh clothes and as clean as a sponge bath could get me, Celeste was perched atop the freight car once more. She nodded her head to me but didn't talk, and I didn't linger in the chilly morning air.

Marcus knelt in front of the figurines I'd created last night, holding up a clear replica of Oliver to examine it in the light of a glowball he'd formed.

"The detail in this is amazing," he said without turning toward me.

"You can have it, if you want." Caught off guard by his praise, I tried to sound dismissive, as if it wasn't one of my finer pieces.

The glowball winked out and he closed his long fingers around the figurine. "Thanks." He grabbed his bag and squeezed past me on his way to the bathroom.

"He's smart," Oliver said after Marcus had left.

"Because he picked the one that looked like you?"

"Yes."

Chuckling, I checked on the dormant gargoyles. They were all weak but stable. It pleased me to see the fox's injuries were healing nicely, and when I checked Oliver, his new patch of clear ruff had striations of red carnelian stretching to the surface. By the time we returned to Terra Haven, all signs of his injury would be healed.

I glanced around at the dormant gargoyles and tried to picture the return trip. Would they be with me? Would they remain in their baetyl? Would they all live through the trip?

Would I?

Marcus returned wearing brown leather pants, thick leather boots, and a lightweight fitted gray cotton shirt with a tiny flame stitched at the high collar. The shirt was regulation FPD attire and woven with protective magic, but the leather pants were new. They hugged his long legs and creaked when he sat on his cot. I glanced down at my unspelled jeans and long-sleeved T-shirt. The comparison between us said more obviously than words how unprepared I was for traversing Reaper's Ridge.

Marcus's attitude had changed to match his clothes, the camaraderie of last night chased away by the sunrise and his familiar scowl back in place. He silently handed me an apple stabbed with a paring knife, half a loaf of bread, and a hunk of soft white cheese. I jerked the knife from the apple and ate the fruit, then concentrated on cutting slices of cheese for each bite of bread. Across from me, Marcus methodically consumed his identical breakfast, seemingly unaffected by the heavy silence choking the air and making it hard to swallow.

"Repairing the baetyl is your job. For everything else, you'll do what I say, when I say it."

I lifted my eyebrows at his high-handed order. Marcus gave me a hard stare, no emotion behind his eyes.

"Is that clear?"

I stuffed a bite of bread into my mouth to choke off a dozen flippant responses and made myself nod. Marcus had experience, training, and more magic than me. It made sense for him to be in charge, especially in the wild magic of Reaper's Ridge. Besides, telling him I'd follow his orders only if I agreed with them wouldn't appease him, and I couldn't afford to have him back out of helping me now.

I'd barely finished eating when the train began to slow.

"Are we there?" Oliver asked.

"Almost."

My stomach tightened around my half-digested breakfast and I ran damp palms down my thighs. I tried to push my fear aside, but it wasn't as easy as last night, when the danger was still a distant prospect. Oliver didn't share my trepidation. The young gargoyle undulated out of the freight car with an excited trill and leapt to the roof. The metal popped under the combined weight of two gargoyles but didn't dent.

Trying to calm myself, I focused on mundane tasks. I tucked my bag up against the larger loading door, folded my blanket on my cot, and laced my boots. The boots were the only part of my outfit that I was sure met Marcus's approval. After our last adventure together, during which a spear of granite had skewered the bottom of my foot straight through my boot, I'd purchased the most heavy-duty pair I could find. They'd been advertised as guard boots and I wore them daily. I hadn't expected to need them, having bought them mainly to counter the remembered pain of the wound, but they'd come in handy twice so far when injured gargoyles had been in too much pain to heed where they stepped.

By the time I'd adjusted the laces from the toe up to the calf on both boots, the train's brakes were squealing and we'd slowed to a crawl. Marcus dropped the air barrier across the broken door, letting in a gentle breeze and the train's perpetual burning-grass odor. I followed him out to the railing, my gaze lifting immediately to the mountains.

Lightning split the clear sky in the distance and thunder rumbled overhead a few seconds later. The tracks ran through a valley filled with sparse, dead weeds and scraggly brush, but a few hundred feet to the west, a dense pine forest blanketed the steep landscape. A gorge dipped into the hillside, revealing a barren ridge of quartz beyond it, the ragged white peaks glowing in the early-morning light. A thick shaft of fire belched from the hill, charring the rocks in its path and extinguishing in a bright explosion made soundless by the distance. Then the train rolled past the gap, and the tree line obstructed the view again.

Pain pinched my hand, and I uncurled my fingers from the railing to examine the red crescent marks of my finger-nail imprints in my palm. When I looked up, Marcus was watching me. I tucked my hands into my armpits.

"We're close. Any change in the gargoyles?" he asked.

I shook my head. "They need to get inside the baetyl." If being near it had been enough, all the gargoyles from this baetyl would have stayed nearby until they recovered.

"Looks like we're really going to Reaper's Ridge, then," he said. "The captain is going to skin me alive when he gets back. Unless we die first."

A falling-down lean-to marked the once bustling Hidden Cache Station. Broken shards of glass lay around the base of the sunken ticket window, and paint flaked from the illegible sign and rotting siding. Weeds grew over extra lines of track that split out into the meadow to multiple neglected loading bays now defined only by thinner patches of weeds. Hidden Cache Station was no longer listed on any rail line, and I had Marcus and his connections to thank again for getting the train to stop here and not another fifty miles up the line at the nearest small town.

The station wasn't empty. A rugged mountain air sled sat well clear of the dilapidated building, a pack of cerberi resting in the sled's shade. The driver hopped from the padded seat to the ground as the train came to a stop. If the station's run-down ticket booth and the mountain range had birthed a human child, the driver would have been their offspring. Wind, sun, and age had weathered his leathery skin into a crush of wrinkles around high cheekbones, a prominent nose, and thin eyes. Dirt caked his heavy pants, and streaks of grime coated a threadbare shirt covering his bony chest and stomach. The old man moved with unexpected agility, though, and clapped a worn cowboy hat to his head before shoving the air sled into position using brute force and a sizable amount of air magic.

Marcus walked back to open the large loading door, and I hopped down to join him. Unlike Emerald Station, this forgotten stop didn't have a platform, which worked in our favor since the air sled hovered at a height only slightly lower than the freight car. We wouldn't have to lift the heavy, dormant gargoyles far to get them loaded.

"The driver's name is Gus," Marcus said, his voice pitched low so only I could hear him. He had arranged for the sled driver to be waiting for us at the station, just as he'd arranged for the freight car to be hitched to the back of the first-class train. I opened my mouth to thank him again, but he continued without giving me a chance. "He's not going to let us load the gargoyles until you pay him."

"The FPD isn't picking up this tab?" I asked, trying to keep the hope out of my voice.

"The FPD has a don't-touch policy regarding Reaper's Ridge. They're not going to fund any portion of any hare-brained expedition involving it."

I clamped my mouth shut before I pointed out the flaw in his logic, since the FPD had already paid for our trip here. If he made me reimburse him for the train car and trip, I'd be in debt to him for the next five years. Besides, I recognized the verbal jab for what it was. Marcus wasn't going to try to talk me out of going to Reaper's Ridge, but it appeared he was done with making things easy.

I grabbed my bag and pulled out a neatly folded bundle of cash, then walked to the front of the sled where Gus was coiling thick bands of earth around twin stone anchors to hold the floating sled in place.

"Hi, I'm Mika," I said.

"Yep." Gus spat to the side.

"How much do I owe you?"

"This'll do." He swiped the cash from my hand and pocketed it without counting the bills.

"But . . . how much—"

"Oh, pardon me, ma'am. Did you want to shop around first?" He swept his arm toward the empty meadow and cackled, the dry sound turning into a wheezy cough.

I'd spent my life's savings when I'd rescued Oliver and

his siblings from Walter at the black magic auction, and Gus had just snatched up every last dollar I'd managed to save since then, including what I'd set aside to pay next month's rent. Unless I sold a record-breaking amount of jewelry in the next week and a half, I was going to have to rely on the goodwill of my landlady to maintain a roof over my head. The thought set my teeth on edge.

I spun on a heel—

And came face-to-jowl with a giant dog's head.

The cerberus huffed a soft bark, its foul breath washing over me and ruffling my hair. Its second head whined and the third sniffed my crotch.

"Whoa, back up," I said, pushing the muzzle from my groin. The whining head licked the side of my face, its tongue as wide as my palm. "Ew!"

Gus guffawed, no help whatsoever.

Oliver coasted from the freight car's roof to my side, and the cerberus backed up a few steps to watch him land, giving me a better look at the three-headed dog. She looked like a Polish hound, with the standard black saddle pattern over an otherwise rich brown coat, but that's where the similarities ended. Aside from having two more heads than a normal dog—all three of them larger than mine—the cerberus was also as tall as a pony and twice as heavy, her body corded with muscles and ending in a whip-long tail that was doing its best to start a windstorm as she crouched to snuffle Oliver. She whined again, or one of her heads did; the other two panted with excitement.

Oliver reared up on his hind legs, which still didn't quite put him at eye level with the cerberus when she stood up.

"Don't be afra—" I started.

Oliver released a trill so high my ears barely registered it, but it made the cerberus go on point. Then the gargoyle rolled onto his back and wriggled his feet at the three-headed hound. She pounced, nipping at his rock body without actually touching him. I ducked the flail of her tail and ran to the far side of the sled. With a few spry steps, Gus joined me.

"Um," I said.

"Never seen a gargoyle play before."

"Is the cerberus playing?" I didn't think her enormous teeth could harm Oliver, but I didn't want to take a chance. I also didn't want her to chip a tooth on Oliver. I couldn't heal a cerberus, and I figured Gus would expect a monetary reimbursement I couldn't afford if she was injured.

"Ginger's gentle as a lamb," Gus said. Ginger growled, three throats in harmony, and snapped her teeth in a fast chatter like bone castanets. Every hair on my body stood on end and I fought to ignore the primitive part of my brain insisting I needed to flee. Oliver wriggled in a circle, trying to imitate the cerberus's eerie chatter. He sounded like a drowning turkey.

Gus watched them tussle for a moment longer before he barked a foreign word. The cerberus leapt to his side and planted her butt nearly on his foot. Gus patted each of her heads. Oliver shook dirt from his back and flapped his wings, giving me a goofy smile I could read far too clearly.

"Cerberi are not city animals," I told him.

"A little help here," Marcus said.

I turned back to the freight car. He'd already transferred two of the lighter gargoyles onto the sled by himself. I scurried to help him with the rest. Gus didn't make a move to help, despite being far stronger than me with air. Sweat ran freely down my face and soaked into my shirt by the time we'd finished, and when Celeste retracted her magical boost, I slumped against the high side of the sled, feeling like I'd run a mile uphill. Marcus looked like he'd taken a stroll by the beach.

He formed a pocket of air and spoke into it, and the weave caught his words, absorbing the sound. After rocketing the air message to the conductor, he shut and latched the freight car. The message zipped into the open side of the engine, where two attendants shoveled manure out the door. Naomi leaned out around them, slinging a message back down the train to Marcus. Her words were for his ears alone, and whatever she said made him grin. I turned away.

The train pulled out of the station while Gus hitched the cerberi to the sled. All six were marked similar enough to Ginger to have been born in the same litter, though the two at the front looked older. Wider than horses—at least from the necks up, where their three heads fanned out from their bulky shoulders—the cerberi had to be staggered along the towline, three to each side. Lined up noses to tail, the pack stretched longer than the freight car, and they looked sturdy enough to pull the sled-load of heavy gargoyles without breaking a sweat.

I started to grab my bag from where I'd tossed it beneath the sled, but when I caught sight of Marcus, I froze. He'd strapped a broadsword to his back, and the black hilt protruded over his right shoulder. The leather harness holding the hilt bisected his chest, and a handful of brass null traps were affixed to the thick straps. A sturdy elemental anchoring rod made of twined copper and quartz hung from a loop at his belt and two slender knife hilts protruded from sheaths in his boots.

He was an FPD fire elemental whose muscular frame topped six feet by several inches. His scowl could cower a kludde. He'd always been intimidating, but I'd gotten used to him. Now he looked like a stranger, and a scary one, at that.

Marcus's hard blue eyes lifted to mine and I forgot how to breathe. A predator looked back at me, but instead of fear, heat washed through my limbs. When he smiled, all teeth and little mirth, I jerked back toward the sled, hefting my bag to the wooden floorboards and climbing in after it. I pretended to double-check the stability of the frozen gargoyles while trying to remember how to breathe normally.

Marcus hopped up to the driver's bench seat beside Gus and settled a crossbow across his lap. Celeste circled on lazy updrafts above us, so high she looked no larger than a thunderbird, but Oliver remained with me. He flapped to the front of the air sled and wormed his way through the dormant gargoyles into a small space behind the driver's bench. I squeezed into the limited space at the back of the cart and sat just as Gus unraveled the earth strands holding us anchored. He loosed a shrill whistle that bumped through five octaves, and the cerberi leaned into their harnesses.

The sled eased forward so smoothly that if my eyes hadn't been open, I wouldn't have known we'd moved. The cerberi transitioned from a walk to a trot to a canter in perfect harmony, enormous paws pounding across the hard soil. Wind whipped through the gargoyles on the open sled, slapping my hair against my face and neck and carrying Gus and Marcus's conversation back to me.

"What's wrong with these ones? Why are they frozen?" Gus asked.

"It's just something that happens to them."

"Must be the rocks for brains." Gus chuckled at his own joke. I scowled at his back.

Gus guided the cerberi to a dirt path at the edge of the long meadow and they veered to follow it, picking up speed. It'd once been a road, but now weeds and trees choked the edges. Sunlight gave way to dappled shadows as the forest closed in around us. Pine and the musky scent of the forest floor filled the air, and above the thunder of paws, I could hear the raucous calls of crows and the occasional shrill challenge of a hawk. The cerberi took the turns of the old road at a gallop, and the sled slid smoothly through the air behind them. It would have been a pleasant experience if not for our destination or the lives of the gargoyles depending on me.

Or Gus.

"How'd a smart FPD man like you get stuck with this tarred-feather task?" Gus asked.

"Wrong place, wrong time."

I switched my glower to Marcus.

"Last I heard, the FPD wised up about Reaper's Ridge."

"It has, but this one"—Marcus tossed a thumb in my direction—"has a plan. She's going to use all these gargoyles to tame the wild magic." His tone said what his words did not: that I was a moron.

I gritted my teeth. Marcus had come up with the cover story. He claimed it was something Gus would believe, was far enough from the truth to keep the baetyl a secret, and would enhance the reputation of gargoyles and gargoyle healers if I "managed to crawl back off this mountain alive."

I waited for Gus's shock or outrage that anyone would think to use a half-dozen helpless gargoyles in such a dangerous manner.

"Why not bring more live ones?" Gus asked. "The boost coming off these is useless."

"Live ones wouldn't come."

Oliver growled, the sound more musical than menacing. I caught his gaze and shook my head. He knew the cover story. He knew Marcus didn't mean what he said. It didn't make it any easier to listen to, though. I stuck my tongue out at the men, and Oliver gave me a weak smile.

"You think it'll work?" Gus asked.

Marcus laughed, and it wasn't a pleasant sound. Gus joined him, shaking his head.

"There's always some crazy city folk who think they can tame the ridge," Gus said. He spat out the side of the wagon, and I threw a shield of air up to block the splatter from hitting me. "Shame they're sending a good company man like you, though."

"I'll be okay. I get paid either way. I just have to get the fool set up, then stand back and watch the fallout."

Gus thought that was hysterical.

I tuned them out and gathered a test pentagram, sliding it into the nearest dormant gargoyle. Her life guttered faintly, with nothing to feed on since the sled's magic was crafted into it and static. I gathered more of the elements, pulling them through the unfocused boost of all seven dormant gargoyles, and grabbed a handful of seed crystals from my bag. The magic I did was less important than letting the gargoyles feed, so I threaded earth through the quartz, reshaping the seeds into a singular sphere, then a diamond, then a snowflake. I kept the quartz in perpetual movement, and to use more magic, I worked as fast as possible, holding the quartz in front of me on a cushion of air that I constantly had to adjust to compensate for the movement of the sled beneath me.

It worked to distract me, too—from Gus and Marcus and anything else they talked about, and from the dwindling distance between us and Reaper's Ridge.

"Stupid girl! Knock that nonsense off before you get us all killed," Gus said.

A wallop of air swung toward the quartz I was working, and I countered it with earth without thinking. Gus's air slapped against my barrier and shattered. He grimaced at the backlash, shooting me a hateful look over his shoulder.

"Get your charge in hand," Gus barked at Marcus.

"Mika. The wild storms are drawn to any active magic. No more for a bit."

I let the quartz drop to my lap. Marcus held the crossbow loose in his hand, a brass null trap affixed to the tip of the notched arrow. His eyes scanned the horizon, the sky, the broken patches of forest, never settling on one place for too long.

Reaper's Ridge rose beside us twice as tall as the road we traveled and separated by a single canyon and a few hardy trees. Storms crawled across the ridge and exhaled from the rocky mountainside into violent snow flurries, explosive lightning and downpours, and fire. Under a cloudless piece of sky, a flash flood gushed across a few hundred feet of hillside before dissipating as suddenly as it had formed. The muddy ground rolled, and new boulders pushed to the surface.

Chills rushed down my body. It was the disaster at Focal Park all over again, only instead of the ridge being divided into five sections of predictable polarized magic, the elements clashed and twisted together in a violent mishmash.

I clutched the edge of the sled and scanned the visible parts of the ridge, hunting for clues to the baetyl's location, but the mountain guarded its secret well.

Gus whistled two short notes, and the sled slowed. I glanced past the cerberi. The overgrown road continued down into the canyon, unobstructed by anything larger than weeds.

"Why are we stopping?" I asked.

"This is as far as I go."

"We're not even to the base of the ridge," Marcus said.

Gus spat over the side of the sled. "This is as far as I go," he repeated.

7

"I hired you to get us to Reaper's Ridge," Marcus said, his voice a menacing rumble as he loomed over the wrinkled old man.

Gus clicked his tongue, and all the cerberi turned toward us, eighteen throats growling in unison. My skin tried to crawl. Oliver stood on his hind legs to see over the driver's bench seat, wings flared in alarm. The cerberi raised their hackles and inched back toward the sled. Gus had dropped an anchor, and we remained in place as they stalked closer.

"Really?" Marcus let out an exasperated breath. "Don't threaten me, old man. I'm not in the mood. If you don't want to go any farther, how much to borrow your team and sled?"

Gus shook his head. "I wouldn't send my least favorite hound to Reaper's Ridge."

"Fine. How much to *buy* the whole pack?"

"Not for sale."

"Not even one?"

"Nope."

Marcus's profile tightened, his standard scowl becoming threatening.

"Get out or I'll dump you out," Gus said. He used a trickle of air to activate a spell woven into the sled, and it began to tilt to the right.

Marcus smacked the spell with a whip of air and the cart righted itself. Gus's gnarled fingers tightened on the reins and his eyes darted across the canyon to the riotous magic. A band of fire and air quested toward us, crackling into fiery lightning before it stretched across the canyon.

"Suit yourself. We're heading back," Gus said.

Marcus clapped a hand over the driver's mouth before he could signal his cerberi.

"How much for the sled?"

When Marcus removed his hand, Gus's grin revealed a few missing teeth. He named an exorbitant price. My heart dropped. I didn't have any more money, let alone the small fortune Gus demanded. Maybe if we carried the gargoyles one at a time, we could make it work. We'd have to move them in stages, making sure we did enough magic around them to keep them alive without doing so much magic as to attract a wild storm.

I eyed the wolf gargoyle. He weighed more than Marcus and me combined. Without using the elements, I wouldn't be able to move him. We needed the sled.

Marcus had already reached the same conclusion, because he was haggling. "Tell you what: I'll accept your price, but only if you agree to pay me half again as much when I sell it back to you."

Gus's eyes shone as he shook Marcus's hand enthusiastically. He snatched up the wad of bills Marcus pulled from his pocket and leapt agilely from the seat to the ground. After unhooking a slender board from the front of the sled, he unhitched the towline from the sled and attached it to the board. When he activated the board's spell, it floated a foot or so off the ground. Gus stepped on, grabbed the reins, and signaled the cerberi with a sharp whistle. They folded back down the line in the direction we'd come. By the time the last cerberus squeezed past the cart, they were galloping. Gus rode the floating board like he'd been air surfing his whole life, and he and his cerberi disappeared back into the forest. In less than a minute, the sound of the cerberi's enormous paws faded and an unnatural silence settled around us, broken only by the rumble of rockslides and thunder across the canyon.

"I don't think he expects you to live long enough to return his sled," I said.

"Easiest money I ever made." Marcus jumped from the driver's seat.

I tried to match his nonchalance as I scrambled to the ground. No birds chirped or called, no squirrels jumped through the branches above us, no lizards scurried through the fallen leaves. If any animals lived this close to Reaper's Ridge, they stayed hidden.

An eagle's shriek echoed off the hills, chased by a clap of thunder. Celeste dove through the trees to land next to me, folding her wings to her black sides as she trotted the last few steps.

"Where is the driver going?" she demanded.

"It doesn't matter. We need to move the sled ourselves," Marcus said. "Mika, set us a new towline."

Gus had taken the original towline with him, but a spare coil of rope was clipped to the underside of the sled. I tied the ends to the eye hooks in the front of the sled, creating a loop of rope.

"Can you pull it?" Marcus asked. He never ceased scanning the surroundings, crossbow and null trap at the ready.

I stepped into the circle of rope and leaned my weight into it. The sled shifted a few inches. Oliver loped to my side and reared to grab the line with his front paws, but his sinuous shape prevented him from getting any leverage and the sled didn't budge. We all turned to Celeste.

"Well?" Marcus asked.

She gave him a hard stare. "I am no animal of burden."

"It's you or me, and I think we'd both prefer me standing guard."

"This is debasing," Celeste grumbled, but she allowed me settle the rope around her broad chest for the same reason she'd trusted me with the secret of baetyls: love. She would do anything to save her mate. With Celeste pulling and me leaning against the back of the sled, we got the platform in motion.

The road switchbacked down into the canyon, and the slant helped us keep momentum through the increasingly dense undergrowth choking the unused path. After flying across the countryside behind the cerberi, our walking pace chafed. It also gave me too much time to think, and a snarl of doubt twisted my thoughts into knots. What if I couldn't repair the baetyl? What if we couldn't find it? How would we feed the gargoyles magic without attracting the storms? What good was my paltry magic against the massive collections of wild, raw elements? Every storm I'd caught a glimpse of could overwhelm me on sheer power alone. What had ever made me think I could do this?

Concussive explosions echoed through the narrowing canyon, the source hidden in the crevices of the mountainside. Every so often, wind howled through the trees, a different temperature every time. I twitched and jumped as I walked, trying to suppress my growing nerves, but the ridge never gave me a quiet moment to gather my wits.

By the time we reached the base of the canyon, I'd switched from cursing Gus for leaving and Captain Monaghan and the rest of the squad for being on vacation when I needed them to counting my blessings. I had Marcus with me, an air sled to move the gargoyles, and Oliver at my side. I wasn't alone. It would be so much worse to face this by myself.

A solid granite bridge arched above the shallow river at the base of the gorge, and Marcus made us wait while he examined it before he allowed us to cross. I would have preferred to test it with earth, but since we didn't want to attract storms, Marcus's visual inspection had to suffice.

I stood at Celeste's shoulder while we waited, studying the thick foliage overgrowing the road on the opposite side.

"You know the way, right?" I asked.

Celeste nodded, and when Marcus gave the go-ahead, she surged up the bank on the other side. I threw my weight against the back of the sled, scrambling after her. After a few dozen feet, she found a marginally clearer path through the dense undergrowth. Another hundred feet up the mountain, it revealed itself to be a real road, widening and clearing as it curved in a switchback.

My footsteps faltered when a wave of dizziness shoved through me. I glanced around, looking for a source. Beside me, Oliver whined.

"It's the ridge," Marcus said. He'd stopped up the trail to let us catch up.

"It feels . . ." I tried to put a term to the irritation grating against my elemental senses. My head felt like I'd been gritting my teeth for hours, the ache at my temples faint but grinding.

"Like a warning against trespassers?" he suggested.

Exactly. The entire mountain hummed with menace.

"We could turn around."

I ran my eyes over the comatose gargoyles. "No. We have to keep going." I stiffened my rubbery knees and pushed back into motion.

No one spoke again, as if being silent could keep us safe. The farther we climbed, the more bizarre and twisted the landscape became until the forest bore no resemblance to the hill across the canyon. Barren patches of scorched earth butted up to sections of woodland so overgrown the trunks of the oaks were bloated and cracked and the underbrush was impenetrable to anything larger than a mouse. Rows of pine trees lying as flat as plowed oat stalks and numerous rockslides only added to the difficulty of traversing the increasingly indiscernible road. Above us, clouds formed, rained, and dissipated in minutes instead of hours or days, often interspersed with lightning and fire. Through it all, the grumbling, cracking, grating sounds of shifting rocks and thunder never let up. I walked on nerves strung so tight I quivered inside my own skin, and when Marcus called a halt, I bounced on my toes.

He raised his crossbow, eyes on the sky and the wild snarl of energy ghosting closer. I jerked around, looking for cover, but we were caught in the middle of a meadow. The safety the trees might have provided was illusory, but being in the open felt foolishly vulnerable.

"What do we do?"

"Nothing. Just be quiet."

Comforting.

The storm was composed of fire wrapped in swirls of air and wood. In other words, it was a perfect firestorm in the making. Flames licked from the raw elemental tangle as if testing the air with a dozen blistering tongues as it swept above the tree line. The pine boughs swayed in its wake, the rustle of needles lost beneath the crackle of the uncontrolled elements.

Holding my breath, I cowered next to the air sled, useless. I couldn't pull magic to protect us without attracting the storm. I didn't have a single nonmagical weapon. I was supposed to be a gargoyle guardian, but I had no way to defend the helpless dormant gargoyles.

"Nobody move," Marcus said, his voice soft. "We might get lucky."

The magic storm slid past us on the outer rim of the meadow. At its current trajectory, it would pass us by without—

The storm kinked on itself, changing course and spearing directly toward us.

"Damn it!" Marcus shot a null trap into the wild energy. It should have neutralized all active magic in the vicinity, but the magic storm swallowed the trap with an infinitesimal hiccup. "Mika, to me!"

I lurched to his side, tripping over my own feet in my rush. Marcus had planted himself between the cart and the storm, and he shoved the anchoring rod into the ground in front of us.

"Link with me," he ordered.

The storm had us in its indifferent sights; hiding our magic had become moot. "With gargoyle help?"

"No gargoyles."

I drew as much as I could hold of water and air, my two weakest elements, then added a balanced amount of earth, fire, and wood and shoved the bundle to Marcus. If I hadn't been so scared, I might have been self-conscious about the pathetic level of magic I offered him.

The link between us snapped into place and Marcus's magic roared through me, so much more powerful than my own. The rush of power tipped my internal awareness into the link, pulling me into the slurry of elements. If I allowed it, the link would consume me, and I'd be as helpless as a dormant gargoyle, just a vessel to pull magic through.

"Relax. You've got this," Marcus said.

I teetered on the precipice of control, then fell back into my body. Magic still flowed between us, but I could separate my core self from the magic.

I opened eyes I hadn't realized I'd closed. Marcus leaned close enough to fill my vision.

"Ready?"

"Ready."

Not a moment too soon. Marcus threw our combined might into a huge shield of water and earth, wrapping it around the sled, the dormant gargoyles, Oliver, and Celeste and tethering it to the elemental anchor he'd pounded into the ground. The magic storm slammed the shield a second later. The impact would have thrown me from my feet, but Marcus grabbed my arm without even looking at me, holding me up.

Water countered fire; earth countered air. The wild magic folded back on itself before twisting for a second attack. Fire and air pounded the shield and burst, unraveling with a thunderous boom. The remaining snarl of wood flared across the shield, feeding from the water, devouring the earth. Fast as thought, Marcus wrapped the wood magic in fire and squeezed. The elements canceled each other out with a clap I barely registered over the ringing in my ears.

Marcus released the link, and I sagged to the ground, drained. He stalked across the quiet meadow and picked up the null trap with a pinch of air. The brass basket was blackened, the previously round shape melted and disfigured. Shaking his head, Marcus tossed the deformed mess into the back of the air sled.

Oliver loped under the sled to my side, rubbing against my forearm with a whine.

"I'm okay. Just catching my breath," I assured him. That hadn't even been a big storm. I tilted my head to peer up the mountain. "Are we close, Celeste?"

"No."

My heart sank.

"That's not going to work many more times," Marcus said, yanking the anchor from the ground and shaking the dirt from it before sliding it back into its loop at his waist.

"We can help," Oliver said, including Celeste in the offer.

"It might be dangerous if the magic backlashes to you," Marcus said before I could.

"No more dangerous than if you burn out before we reach the baetyl," Celeste said. "Rourke is getting weaker. We need to keep moving." She leaned her chest into the rope and dug her back paws into the soil. Marcus pushed the sled until she got it in motion again. I braced my hands on the dirt and shoved to my feet. Another ten minutes' rest would have been preferable. Marcus picked up his crossbow and notched another null trap—whatever good it would do us.

"If we use the dormant gargoyles, it'd help them at least," I said, falling into step with him. "The anchor worked, right?"

Everything had happened so fast, I had only an impression of the anchor funneling some of the wild magic harmlessly into the soil.

"More than the trap."

"What about the sword? Does it have any special properties?"

"Against raw elements, no. But if we encounter something with a body, it might come in handy."

"Do you really think anything could live here among the storms?"

He shrugged. "I've seen stranger things."

We climbed the switchbacks as fast as Celeste could pull the sled. My thighs ached and my stomach sat heavy with fear and doubt. Marcus sent Oliver to scout the way in the air, and I bit my tongue to hold in my protests. Oliver was smart and fast; he wouldn't put himself in danger. Even so, after he flew off, I spent so much time looking at the sky that my neck knotted and my toes bruised inside my boots from tripping over unnoticed rocks.

Our luck held for almost a half hour, until a small storm of raw water and air spinning as tight as a tornado veered off its previously straight course and whirled toward us. It switched directions so rapidly, we didn't have time to move from where we were pinned between a steep outcrop of ragged milky quartz and a washout. Already past the storm, Oliver circled back, wings beating so fast they blurred in his effort to reach us.

"No, don't let him—"

Marcus formed an air message and curved it around the storm. I half expected the wild magic to snatch it out of the air or change course in attraction to the magic, but it didn't alter its headlong rush for us.

I thrust my magic toward Marcus without taking my eyes from Oliver. Our linking was rough but fast, and in my worry for Oliver, it didn't unseat my equilibrium. When the message reached Oliver, he pulled up, his long body sagging beneath his spread wings. I let out a shaky breath.

"Thank you." Oliver was clear of the storm. He would be safe.

If Marcus replied, a gust of wind took his words. He formed another shield, this one fire and earth, and anchored it in the copper and quartz rod he stomped into the ground. I could feel the dormant gargoyles in our link this time, but Marcus didn't include Celeste despite her silent offer of enhancement. I could have accepted her boost and pulled more magic into the link, but I trusted Marcus to have a plan.

The storm dipped, coating the ground beneath it in ice and lifting rocks and weeds into a funnel. Wide-eyed, I watched the frozen front race toward us. Marcus locked my wrist in his hand and drew a wallop of power from our link, altering the fire in the shield from the basic elemental form to the weaves for a white-hot heat. When the storm hit us, it melted into nothing with an anticlimactic *shush* of released air.

"That's more like it," Marcus said. He released me from the link at the same time he let go of my arm, and I sagged against the sled. My heavy breaths fogged the chilled air, and between ragged pants, I could hear the tinkle of the ice crystals melting in the sunlight. Marcus rolled a weak band of heat across the ground in front of Celeste, thawing it, and we pushed back into motion.

Before following the sled, Marcus stooped to grab something from the icy ground. It wasn't until he held it up that I recognized the frosted twist of metal as a null trap.

"How did that get there?"

"I tossed it. I hoped if it was grounded, it would work. I think it's safe to say they're useless."

"That storm should have passed us by," I said, pulling the grounding rod from the ground. It burned my palm, and

I bounced it between my hands to cool it until Marcus took it.

"It's as if someone is guiding these damn things toward anything living," Marcus said.

I shuddered at the thought. "Not anything. It ignored Oliver."

In unison, we glanced at the sled of dormant gargoyles.

"It's them," I said.

I couldn't believe I'd missed it. It was so obvious. The mining explosion, the broken baetyl: They were the same thing.

"Because the gargoyles are basically leaking magic?" Marcus guessed.

I shook my head. "Celeste, why haven't any of the other baetyls been accidentally discovered?"

"Baetyls protect themselves."

Exactly. The Native Americans had avoided Waupecony Ridge long before the storms. The baetyls must have some form of a ward or protection spell to scare off anyone who ventured too close. But the lure of wealth had spurred the members of the Hidden Cache Mining Company to ignore the dangers.

"The early miners, they merely lost their memories, right?" I said, without giving Marcus a chance to respond. "They must have gotten too close, and the baetyl's protective measures kicked in. The storms didn't start occurring until the incident with the Hidden Cache mine. Baetyls have their own type of magic—"

"They *are* magic," Celeste interrupted.

"What if the miners broke *into* the baetyl and fractured its magic? All these wild storms have to be coming from somewhere. What if it's coming from the baetyl?"

"That would explain a lot," Marcus said.

"I think so, too. And if the dormant gargoyles are tuned to this specific baetyl's magic, then these wild storms might also be tuned to them. The gargoyles might actually attract the storms."

"Well, doesn't this day just keep getting better," Marcus said to no one in particular.

———

THE THIRD MAGIC STORM WHIRLED ACROSS A BARREN SLOPE OF Reaper's Ridge and headed straight for us less than five minutes later. Oliver whistled a warning, giving us time to stop on a plateau of sandstone before the storm rolled over a gully into view, its snaking coils of earth and water covering over eighty feet of ground and moving so fast we had no chance of escape. It ripped up the ground, spewing gravel in its wake and hurtling hail in every direction. The few spindly trees in its path cracked and splintered.

"It's too big," I said. My knees felt like wet sand, and I locked them. "If we try to shield against it, it'll flatten us."

"We need to weaken it."

"How?"

"Unravel it. Come on." Marcus grabbed my hand and pulled me into a stumbling run *toward* the oncoming storm.

"What are you doing?!"

"Giving us a head start. Link up."

I thrust magic to him as I finally got my feet under me. He didn't slow our sprint until the pebble-size hail stung our faces.

"Concentrate on earth," he said. "Anywhere it's wrapped around water, loosen it."

"Me? Don't you want to do it?"

"It's your element. Get to work."

"But . . ."

"Unless you want to let it hurt the gargoyles."

I grabbed hold of the link. The elements came in a rush, enhanced by the dormant gargoyles and Marcus. His magic signature—a rosewood shield wrapped in flames and sparks of lightning—sat in my head with the same solid, comforting presence as his fighter's stance at my side.

Reaching for the first cable of wild earth felt like sticking my hand into a fire and trying to grab a particular flame. The raw element writhed around my magic, eating away my control. I sliced it, cutting a piece of earth from the bundle. The severed end dissipated.

"Just like that. Keep going. Don't stop, no matter what."

Working on the outer perimeter of the storm where I had a remote chance of seeing what I was doing, I hacked twists of earth as fast as I identified them. With the snarl of water and earth swallowing the hillside, I had no shortage of options, but no matter how fast I sliced through the earth strands, more always took their place, many of which were too tightly bound to the writhing water to budge.

I faltered for only a second when Marcus scooped me up, then redoubled my efforts as he retreated.

"It's not going to be enough." We were almost to the sled, and though I'd reduced the storm to one-tenth its original size, it loomed twice as large as the first storm we'd tackled. It hadn't slowed, either. Hail battered us, the tiny beads of ice sharp as finger flicks against my exposed face and hands. I squinted against the dust and sand, holding a hand over my eyes to shield them.

Dipping into our linked magic, Marcus enclosed our upper bodies in an air bubble, shielding us from the elements. Without setting me down, he pulled the anchor rod from its loop at his waist and hurled it into the ground, stamping it into place.

"My turn," Marcus said, tugging on the power of the link. I relinquished it in time for him to wrap a shield of fire and water around us, Celeste, and the cart of gargoyles. It wouldn't be enough, but we didn't have another option.

8

T he storm slapped against the shield and shattered it in a single blow, hurtling Marcus and me into the air. We slammed to the ground a half-dozen feet from the sled.

Wild magic pinged between the helpless dormant gargoyles, battering them with stones and hail. Celeste fought free of the rope and the storm, scrambling up the hillside to safety.

The storm should have swept over the cart and continued across the ridge, but it didn't. With almost predatory focus, it attacked the dormant gargoyles. Desperate, I seized control of the magic in the link again and resumed my assault on the storm, slashing and yanking on the tangles of earth.

When I grabbed a strand that pulsed like tainted quartz, I cropped it, shocked. The rest of the wild magic had been pure, undiluted earth. This was tuned—malignant and sharp, but tuned. I scrambled to find it again, and this time I cut through the flawed magic with a sharp slash.

The last of the wild water flattened, and the storm

billowed above the dormant gargoyles like a fluffed sheet, then settled onto them and disappeared.

I collapsed. Marcus grunted when my head hit his chest. I froze, taking a quick assessment of my location. Crap. I'd landed on top of him when the storm blasted us.

"Oh! Are you okay?" I asked, rolling to the side. Gravel bit into my hands and knees.

"Fine." He groaned as he sat up. I pushed to my feet and gave him a hand to help him up. Considering he weighed twice as much as me, it was more a token offering than actual help.

"Sorry about that. Again." This wasn't the first time an explosion had ended up with me using him as a cushion. I circled him, remembering the injuries he'd sustained when he'd protected me in Focal Park. The spell in his shirt had held this time, and his back was merely dirty. "I didn't plan on making it a habit."

He snorted and drew his sword, checking its length. I winced in sympathy at the bruise its sheath had probably left on his back. His shirt wouldn't have protected against that.

I stumbled back to the gargoyles, two inches of hail crunching underfoot. I tested all seven twice before I believed my readings.

"They're okay," I said. Cut up and abraded from the flying rocks, but their internal balance wasn't skewed, as I'd feared.

"They're better than okay. They're stronger."

I glanced at Marcus, surprised by his accurate guess, then realized we hadn't broken our link. Letting our connection unravel, I said, "I felt something in the storm. At the end. Did you catch it?"

"The repulsive bit of earth?"

"I think it was the baetyl's warped magic."

"That makes sense. If all these storms are coming from the baetyl, they should be tainted with it."

"It fits with our theory of why the storms are attracted to the dormant gargoyles."

"Rourke hasn't been this healthy in years," Celeste said, showering us with sand and ice when she shook out her wings.

After getting her permission, I checked her with a tuned blend of the elements. Celeste had a few scratches but was otherwise unharmed.

"You can heal me when Rourke is safe," she said when I reached for a seed crystal.

"She's right. Conserve your strength." Marcus scanned the broken terrain. "Are we close, Celeste?"

"About halfway there."

I slumped against the side of the sled, eyeing the steep ascent ahead of us.

"This is good news, Mika," Marcus said, taking in my tired expression. "The energy in storms doesn't hurt the gargoyles, not like it would us. Plus, the gargoyles do a great job of making the storms predictable. That means we can switch strategies, which is damn lucky. Defense isn't working; we're going on the offense."

We put Marcus's new plan into action with the next storm—this one a whirlwind of water, wood, and air. It barreled down on us in the middle of a scorched gully where burned stumps and fallen logs had slowed our progress to an aggravating creep. Celeste ducked out of the rope and took to the air before the storm reached us, and Marcus used the anchor rod to pin the sled in place. Then we sprinted toward the storm again, angling up the hill out of its path.

"Same as last time: Cut the storm apart, but this time focus on air," Marcus ordered.

I nodded. He was playing to my strengths: In the destructive cycle of the elements, earth destroyed air. He could use fire against water and wood with more efficiency than I could.

"Should we link?" I asked.

"No. We'll be more efficient apart."

Holding a stitch in my side, I watched the seething magic tumble across the ground. Chunks of ash puffed into the air whenever the storm touched down, lifted by the storm's wind and the plants bursting from the soil. Sporadic showers fell from the midst of the energy, and the rich aroma of freshly churned soil and rain drifted through the air. It was almost a shame to break apart this storm; it left a string of plants in its wake, rejuvenating the otherwise barren hillside.

Well before the storm was close enough for me to reach, Marcus tore into its outer edges, burning through the wood element. I tapped a foot impatiently, useless until Celeste landed close enough to offer me a boost. I grabbed at the magic she offered and flung earthen blades into the vortices of air.

Despite our assault, the storm bounded toward the dormant gargoyles, picking up speed until it pounced, frothing around their frozen shapes. Plants erupted from the soil, growing taller than the sides of the sled in seconds, but they couldn't obscure the wild magic from us. Methodically, we slashed it to pieces until it weakened enough to unravel on its own. I jogged back to the sled even as I tested the gargoyles. They all felt the same as before: stronger than they'd been in Terra Haven but still comatose.

"Not too shabby," Marcus said with his first real smile of the day.

The storm had shifted a few gargoyles on the sled, and we set them back in place. Then Marcus cut through the vines and small trees choking the sled, and we pushed onward.

We weren't so lucky with all the storms. Most were more violent, tearing up earth, striking with lightning, belching flames and ice alike. But our strategy was sound. Fatigue proved to be a greater obstacle. The higher we climbed, the more frequently we were forced to stop to deal with the storms. Oliver returned to my side to give me a boost, but even with his help, every encounter drained my energy, and my sprints toward the oncoming storms became jogs. In between storms, my feet dragged along the path. I ate the snacks Marcus handed me. I drank the water he gave me. I focused on not tripping. Only the dormant gargoyles and their improved health kept me going.

The dead gargoyle beside the trail caught me completely off guard. She was small and looked like a cross between a hedgehog and a wolverine, though twice the size of either animal. Her butterfly wings were spread as if to catch the sun, but her body had faded to gray and her right side had eroded into the dirt. I fell to my knees beside her and tried to help her anyway, but my gargoyle-tuned magic didn't penetrate the dead rock.

With trembling fingers, I brushed a layer of dirt from her face. She had been so close to her baetyl, and she had died. Alone. Her life fading until nothing but the husk of her body remained.

I'd begun to hope that if we unraveled enough wild magic, the pieces of the baetyl inside it would fill the dormant gargoyles on the sled with life and they'd wake, but staring into the lifeless gray eyes of the dead gargoyle, I knew it wouldn't be enough. Nothing short of fixing the baetyl would be enough.

Oliver whined and twined around me, tugging me from the corpse.

"Come on. There's nothing we can do for that one," Marcus said.

"Shouldn't we do something? I don't know—bury it?"

"It is customary to scatter the body," Celeste said. I glanced toward the old gargoyle. She hadn't stopped. The trail was steeper here and momentum was precious. She plodded past, head bowed.

"Is it okay if I do that?"

"It's part of your duties as a healer and guardian," she said.

My heart squeezed. I gathered earth and wood and wrapped the deceased gargoyle. The body crumbled under the weave, the once life-filled quartz disintegrating into pieces no larger than sand. With a boost from Oliver, I lifted the remains on a current of air and scattered them across the hill. Oliver hummed a sorrowful note, and Celeste added high-pitched harmony.

Swiping tears from my lashes, I pushed to my feet.

The hedgehog-wolverine was only the first of many dead gargoyles we found along the ridge. I stopped counting them after a dozen, and it sickened me how quickly I perfected the magic to decompose their bodies and scatter them. I began to look forward to the storms. Those at least I could do something about.

Heart weary and exhausted, I didn't understand why we stopped under a clear sky with no storm on the horizon until Celeste spoke.

"This is the entrance to the baetyl."

We'd made it? We'd survived Reaper's Ridge? Relief swamped me, followed by a wave of nausea as I realized that deep down, I hadn't expected to make it. I bent in half, taking deep breaths until my innards settled back in place.

When I was sure my shaking legs would hold me up, I fumbled around the sled to look at the entrance. Cut into the steep hillside and shadowed by a rocky overhang, the crooked opening was no wider than my outstretched arms and thoroughly unimpressive. I would have walked right past it without noticing if Celeste hadn't pointed it out.

"This is it? It's so . . . accessible. Anyone could walk right in." All gargoyles had wings. Why wasn't the entrance somewhere only they could reach?

"Normally, humans wouldn't be able to get this close. Thank you." The last was for Marcus, who had lowered anchors on the sled to take the burden from Celeste.

Summoning my energy, I jogged up the incline. A ledge of unnaturally flat ground lay in front of the opening, and the rest of the hill above us was too steep to traverse. The baetyl entrance itself was nothing to look at, but when I turned around, the view took my breath. Reaper's Ridge fell away beneath us, ravaged and misshapen, giving way to a view of the lush rolling foothills and the valley farther away. If I had wings, it would have been easy to launch into the sky.

Oliver landed next to me and peered inside the dark opening. His ruff flattened and he backed up so quickly he tripped over his hind legs and crashed to his side.

"Oliver!" I reached for him, but he'd already scrambled to his feet. Turning, he barreled into me, knocking me to the side of the entrance and pinning me against the slope.

"Something's coming! Something big!" he cried.

I sprawled against the rock slope, trying to catch my

footing. Before I found my voice to ask what he meant—
nothing big would fit through the opening—Marcus
sprinted to the opposite side of the entrance, tossing the null
traps into the cave. Using a spear of earth magic to drill a
hole, he plunged the battered anchor rod into the rock in
front of the cave.

"Celeste, to me," he ordered. He flattened himself
against the rock face across the baetyl opening from me.
"Storm or beast?" he demanded.

"Storm," Oliver said, releasing me. I staggered at my
sudden freedom and braced a hand on the hill to steady
myself.

"I can feel the energy building," Celeste said.

"Do we have time to move the sled?" Marcus asked.

As if in answer, the ridge shook, raining pebbles onto
our heads. Beneath my hand, the rock heated and reshaped.
Fear flooded me with a burst of energy and I scrambled
back, Oliver at my side. When I reached for the elements,
his boost was already there, waiting for me.

Marcus threw a five-element ward across the opening,
anchoring it into the rod and tying it off.

"Ready?" he asked. Anticipation tightened his features
and lit his eyes.

"I hope so."

Wild magic burst through the ward, tearing it to shreds
and shattering the rod. The concussion knocked me to my
butt and robbed me of my hearing. Marcus caught himself
on a knee and stayed there, ripping into the magic as it
emerged. It swelled from the baetyl to fill the sky, endless
writhing bands of destructive raw elements building into a
deadly monstrosity.

In a stomach-dropping rush, it dove back to the earth
and swallowed us.

9

The earth pitched beneath me, and I rolled to the right, narrowly avoiding being swallowed by the shifting ground. Without rising, I slashed through twists of earth and wood, destroying the elements nearest me. The hillside stabilized, but I couldn't catch my breath; fire and water rolled in a tight mass of lung-scalding steam. Lashing out, I cut the loose coils of writhing fire. A deluge of water spilled from the storm, soaking me, and I sucked in cool oxygen.

The storm dwarfed all we'd encountered along the way. It wasn't two or three elements but all five bunched together, creating mayhem. The violent magic wouldn't boost the gargoyles until we could unravel it, and in the meantime, it ricocheted between them, knocking their frozen bodies into each other. I struggled to rise and protect them, but layers of wild magic pinned me to the hillside.

Rocks surged and grew behind me, burying Oliver in a pile of sand and stones. Frantic, I snapped a dozen strands of earth where they touched the ground around him, and he burst free, shaking grit into the air. A spear of wood element lanced from the storm as if aiming for me. I lurched to the side, narrowly evading the wild magic. It plowed into the soil, sprouting a two-foot sapling in a spray of rocks and dirt. Shielding my eyes with a hand, I burned through the tangle of wood before it could bury the ledge in a new forest, then rolled back to Oliver's side. His eyes were as wide as an owl's and he trembled as he curled around me.

Seeing his fear cut through my own panic. He was depending on me for protection. If I continued to react instead of attack, we wouldn't survive. I needed to think like a guardian.

"I'll keep us safe," I promised. "Stay close."

I concentrated on our immediate vicinity, unraveling earth and dousing fire, refusing to let any of the storm touch the ground near us. Across the ledge from us, Marcus did the same, holding a storm-free bubble around himself and Celeste. He wielded massive bands of the elements, slicing through fire more often than any other element. Taking my cue from him, when I had a chance to pick my next attack, I struck at earth; it was my strongest element and, after fire, the most deadly.

Snow and sand blinded me, winds knocked me flat and lifted me from the ground, and fire scorched me more than once. I fought through it all, hunting for the disharmonious quartz-tuned knot of earth holding the whole storm together. The wild magic blurred into a huge, shape-changing monster, and my control of my magic slipped and fumbled with weariness. Occasionally an explosive blaze or a sheet of ice forced me to shield Oliver and myself, but I dropped my barriers as soon as it was safe. Defending would do nothing but tire me out—attacking was the only option.

I whittled away the storm's power with increasingly

clumsy strokes, and when I found the snarl of quartz-tuned earth, it was pure happenstance. I pounced, clinging to it with strength born of desperation. As fast as I could finagle my fatigued magic, I tore it apart. The wild elements collapsed and dispersed in a harmless gust of warm air.

A hush fell over the ridge, broken only by the harsh sounds of my panting followed by the chatter of my teeth when a chilly breeze plastered my soaked clothes to my body.

It took a moment for me to focus on Marcus. Dark circles cupped his eyes and exhaustion weighted his shoulders. He swiped mud from his leather pants as he stood, hail falling from his shoulders when he bent forward. The spell in his shirt had kept his torso dry and clean, a fact I envied as my body convulsed in another shiver. I'd managed to get to my knees at some point, and dirty snow melted around my calves. With reddened fingers, I sluiced slush from my thighs.

Plucking at my shirt to peel the wet fabric from my skin, I sought out Celeste. She'd flown to the sled where it sat on the ground, the spells previously holding it aloft destroyed by the wild magic. The taller gargoyles had toppled, including Rourke, and she used her talons to right him. Her lack of alarm told me most of what I needed to know—he was okay.

For now.

"Are you hurt?" Marcus asked. He loomed over me. I tilted my head back to look at him, but the muscles in my neck didn't cooperate and my head lolled toward my shoulder. Damn, I was tired.

"Sleep would be nice." If there were time. We didn't know how long this reprieve would last. Reaching deep into myself, I found the strength to stand. Oliver squirmed to his feet, stretching his wings, and I realized he'd been propping me up. I reached for him, and he brushed his head against my fingertips before coasting down the short incline to the dormant gargoyles.

"We need to go into the baetyl now, before the energy has a chance to build again," I said. I wouldn't survive a second mega-storm.

Marcus's jaw muscles bunched. Grit pulled his dark hair into wayward spikes, and I thought the tousled look suited him far more than his scowl.

"You think that's wise?" he asked.

My head pounded. "No. But I don't think we have a choice. Let me check on the gargoyles, then we'll go."

"You can't even walk."

He issued the statement like a challenge. Giving him a scowl as fierce as the one he leveled on me, I straightened and took a step. My boot caught in the mud and the suction threw off my fragile balance. Marcus caught me when I stumbled into him. I glared at his Adam's apple, daring him to say something. He didn't. Shifting his grip to my bicep, he marched me down the slope to the gargoyles. I forced some rigidness into my backbone and dredged up the rest of my reserves so I could stand unaided when he released me. Unimpressed, Marcus crossed his arms, as if waiting to watch me face-plant.

I tottered between the gargoyles, checking for injuries. Internally, they all were remarkably strong, and their renewed health breathed a modicum of energy into me. I couldn't run a mile, or really even run at all, but I could do this; I could repair the baetyl. For them. To save seven lives.

I had to.

The gargoyles' physical injuries were minor—nicks and scrapes where their paralyzed bodies had slammed and rattled into each other during the storm. Normally I would have pulled out seed crystals and healed them, but saving my strength was more important. I could feel the sluggishness of my magic; expending it now, even to ease the small pains in their bodies, would be foolish. I didn't right those who had toppled for the same reason.

I checked Oliver, then Celeste, relieved to find them basically unharmed. Celeste had the equivalent of bruises along her hip and back and Oliver felt weary, but they would both survive without any assistance on my part.

Taking a deep breath, I turned to face the baetyl opening. The ledge had been completely reshaped by rockslides and new stone and plant growth, but the baetyl's opening was unchanged. I took it as a good sign. At least some of the baetyl's powers remained to protect it.

"Okay, I'm ready," I said.

"Really."

It wasn't a question, and when I met Marcus's gaze, I found anger rather than skepticism.

"Can you even get back up to the ledge?" he asked.

Frowning, I wrapped my arms around myself for warmth. What had put a burr in his britches? "Are you going to test me every step of the way?"

"I'm not here to carry you." His hands flexed into fists, then relaxed. "Why didn't you contact me before yesterday?"

My eyebrows shot up at the non sequitur. Maybe I'd misheard him. "What?"

"After Focal Park. I can tell when someone is interested in me, so don't try to lie. You were interested. I made it clear all you had to do was come find me, but you never made a move."

"You want to talk about . . . about if I like you? Now?" My face heated under his glower.

"Yes."

"But—" I glanced toward the baetyl, willing to attempt a jog up the hill if it would extricate me from what was fast becoming an embarrassing conversation.

"I want an answer."

"Of course I liked you, but I was searching for a cure for the dormant gargoyles. There wasn't time . . ." My reason was perfectly valid, but telling Marcus to his face that I hadn't had time for him seemed callous. Besides, after the first few weeks of nonstop searching hadn't unearthed a cure, I thought I'd already missed my chance with him. A man like Marcus didn't have to wait around for women, and I'd told myself that whatever he'd seen in me that day in Focal Park wouldn't have been enough to hold his attention after the excitement died down. His ambivalence toward me on this trip had confirmed my prediction. Except now he acted as if I'd offended him. Had I hurt his feelings?

"Right. I should have realized that," he said.

"Thank you." The knot in my stomach eased.

"I mean, why bother making time for a life when you're so intent on killing yourself?"

He delivered the question in such an understanding tone that it took me a moment to process the words.

"What are you talking about?"

"This. This is what I'm talking about." He jabbed a finger at me and frustrated disdain replaced all the false sympathy in his expression. "You can barely stand up straight, but you're ready to rush off to the next danger. You've got no regard for your life."

"That's nonsense. I'm not trying to kill myself. I'm trying to save lives."

"Then act like it."

"What's that mean?" The wind no longer felt quite so

cold, and I shifted from hugging myself to mirroring Marcus's crossed-arm stance.

"You hunt out ways to throw yourself into danger. You want examples? We're standing on Reaper's Ridge—"

"We just defeated Reaper's Ri—"

"And what about that stunt you pulled in Focal Park?" he asked, his words overpowering mine. "You were so eager to meet death, you practically ran to it."

"Someone had to break the null."

His ugly chuckle set my teeth on edge.

"The null. Right. I hadn't even gotten to that. I was talking about when you split your spirit among five different gargoyles and nearly liquefied your brain. But you just made my point. You think saving others means rushing into every dangerous situation you see—"

"Isn't that your job?" I shot back, irritated that he made me feel like I needed to defend myself. Of all people, he should understand.

"I'm a Federal Pentagon Defense warrior. I have training. I have full-spectrum strength."

"So that makes it okay? I'm a guardian. The *only* guardian these gargoyles have. Of course I'm going to take risks to save their lives."

"Taking a risk is one thing; swapping your life for a gargoyle's is another."

I clenched my jaw. Some people valued human lives more highly than gargoyles', but I never expected the elitist attitude from Marcus. "Is your ego so fragile that you would have preferred I let gargoyles die so I could have spent time fawning over you?"

"Don't pretend you believe I'm that shallow."

"You don't have a monopoly on being a savior, Marcus. The gargoyles need me. I'm the only person who has a chance at saving them. And you know what? If it means my life—*one* life—has to be sacrificed to save *seven*, then so be it." Hearing my own conviction sent a tremor through my knees, but I didn't take the words back.

"That's just it. Being a healer—being a *guardian*," he corrected before I could, "doesn't mean your life is a bargaining chip."

"It means I'll do whatever I have to to save the gargoyles."

"This is why I said no," he said softly, making me realize we'd been shouting. "You don't have the good sense to save yourself. And it's why I said yes, because I couldn't let you kill yourself without trying to stop you."

"Are you saying you're going to try to prevent me from going into the baetyl?" I glanced around, locating Oliver and Celeste. They watched from a few feet away. Celeste's face was unreadable, but Oliver looked scared.

Marcus shook his head. "No. I'm not stopping you. Just..." He rubbed his hand across his mouth and jaw, his stubble rasping audibly in the charged silence. The tension left his shoulders and a pitying look replaced his scowl. "Just think about what I've said. The gargoyles don't need a martyr; they need a guardian *and* a healer."

He turned away to rummage in his pack, and I glared at his back. I couldn't decide what pissed me off more: the fact that he thought the lives of gargoyles weren't worth as much as mine or that he thought my actions to save them were rash.

Another breeze swept the hillside, and I ground my teeth together to stop their chattering. Every single scrap of me had been soaked, and even though it felt as if my blood were boiling, I wasn't getting any drier.

"Here," Marcus said, his voice as flat as his expression.

He poured an unmarked packet into a canteen, swished it, then thrust the canteen into my hands. "Drink it all."

I sniffed the opening and pulled my head back with a grimace when a nauseating odor of brine, algae, and something bitter made my nostrils try to pinch together. "What is it?"

"A stimulant."

I glanced up at his cold eyes and took a sip, gagged, and doubled over coughing.

"It's not wine. Chug it. Try not to breathe between drinks and it won't be so bad."

Eyes watering, I forced myself to raise the canteen again and took a massive swallow. My throat threatened to close, but I powered through.

Marcus dumped a packet of the pungent powder directly into his mouth. With a band of air, he pulled a water bottle from the sled to his hand, took a gulp, swished, and swallowed. My tongue curled in sympathy for his assaulted taste buds.

"Ugh. I have the breath of a swamp monster," I muttered. I rubbed my tongue against the roof of my mouth, but it didn't alleviate the nasty flavor.

"Better than the breath of a burned-out null."

I rolled my eyes, but my frustrated comeback evaporated as energy surged through my veins. I raised my hands to stare at them, half expecting to see them glowing, but they remained reddened and dull. I took a step on legs that had transformed from pudding back to muscle and experimentally pulled the elements to me. They came in a rush.

"This is amazing." I jumped up and down. My mind, body, and magic felt as fresh as if I'd had a week off.

Without warning, Marcus sent me stumbling with a blast of heated air that pulled the moisture from my clothing and dried me at the same time. I closed my eyes against the stinging wind but didn't protest. When he finished, I was chapped but dry and warm. My smile seemed to irritate him, if the tick of his jaw muscle was any indication. I grinned wider.

"Stop bouncing," he ordered. "This isn't a game. We still don't know if you can fix a baetyl. We could be walking into a trap, so keep your wits sharp."

"Oh, good advice," I said, my voice heavy with cheery sarcasm. Giving him a flippant response was easier than letting his words sink in. The scary unknown of the broken baetyl loomed in my imagination, feeding my fears. Psyching myself out about it wouldn't help. "You know me. Always running into danger without a thought. But since you're telling me to be cautious . . ."

Marcus swiveled his head to glare at me, and the words died in my throat. I spun on a heel and marched up the incline to the tunnel entrance.

Peering into the dark opening, it was harder to maintain a sense of detachment from my fear. The wild storms had all but drained me. My arms were cut, my legs and feet bruised. I'd been burned and frozen. And that had only been what had escaped the baetyl. What horrors lurked inside?

————

MARCUS INSISTED ON GOING FIRST AND CELESTE FELL IN AT his heels. Oliver and I trailed after them, and I wondered if Marcus could feel the heat of my glare between his shoulder blades. Our moody leader also insisted I conserve my strength for whatever was ahead, so all five glowballs illuminating the tunnel were his. The walls were rough and asymmetrical, run through with veins of quartz and shale. Only the floor was smooth, polished by thousands of stone footsteps. I expected a challenge around every bend—a physical obstacle or more storms—but we strolled into the mountain without issue.

The cool air grew more humid the deeper we went, until moisture clung to the rock walls and dripped on our heads from the ceiling.

"It's too cold," Oliver said, his chiming voice hushed. I shivered at the creepy *shush-shush* echoes of his words.

"Is it supposed to be this wet?" I asked.

"Yes."

Marcus's back stiffened and he halted at a turn in the tunnel. Celeste crowded up next to him and he stepped aside to make room. My feet ground to a halt beside her. We'd found the baetyl.

Marcus's glowballs illuminated a field of citrine crystals barely as tall as my hand and packed more densely than blades of grass across the sloped floor. Darkness swallowed the rest of the cavern to our left and right, but bulky shapes loomed beyond the light. Squinting, I could make out flat planes and sharp angles, and when my brain put the pieces together, I gasped in wonder.

The baetyl was *filled* with crystals.

Six-sided prisms longer and thicker than a freight car crisscrossed the baetyl at the edge of the light, overlapping compact crystals no larger than Celeste. Even smaller crystals filled the gaps, and everywhere I looked glistened as endless facets caught and reflected the glowballs' fiery light.

"It's so dark. It's worse than I feared," Celeste said.

I reached for fire to form a glowball, and it flickered and wobbled before steadying into a sphere of light. Even then, the element stretched, skewing the light.

The warp of the baetyl was in full effect.

"Careful," Marcus said when I pushed the glowball into the cavern.

The light twisted, the element growing harder to control across the distance. Shadows guttered along the geometric lines of the baetyl, giving shape to crystal-coated alcoves and ledges of every color and type of quartz. The shifting golden light made the tigereye and agate crystals appear to ripple like liquid, and the jewel-bright spears of amethyst, citrine, prasiolite, and rose quartz refracted their colors across smoky quartz and shimmering clear crystals. The alien structure looked like the inside of a mountain-size geode, and the beauty of it stole my breath.

Even the air felt different, smooth and ancient. The humidity of the tunnel gave way to a cooler texture with a scent as unique as the baetyl. Part undisturbed earth, part weighted air, and part mineral, the odor pooled in the back of my throat, and I took deep breaths to savor the aroma. It was the smell of pure quartz—and up until that moment, I hadn't even known quartz had a smell, let alone that I had been craving it.

In the clutter of quartz and dense shadows beyond my glowball, I couldn't determine the boundaries of the baetyl, but Celeste's comparison of its size to Focal Park seemed about right.

The glowball twisted out of my grasp and imploded in a burst of sparks. Darkness coated the baetyl once more, hiding all but the tiny bubble of space Marcus's lights illuminated. I smoothed my hands down my thighs.

"Now what?" Marcus asked.

I don't know, sprang to my lips, but Marcus already knew I didn't know what I was doing. I wasn't going to give him the satisfaction of saying it out loud.

"We keep going," I said.

I contemplated the lawn of jagged crystals covering the floor. The baetyl had never been intended for fragile human bodies. Every surface had a sharp point. Tentatively, I tested the sole of my boot on the uneven peaks. When the crystals didn't puncture the tread, I settled my weight onto my foot and took another step. The crystals held firm.

Oliver stepped onto the quartz and hissed. Beside him, Celeste touched a crystal with a talon and narrowed her eyes.

"It hurts," Oliver said. He spoke so softly that I didn't think he meant for me to hear.

"You can wait—" My words died in my throat at Oliver's fierce glower. He must have been learning that look from Marcus.

"I go where you go," he said.

His tone was pure Marcus, too. I glanced to the fire elemental to see if he noticed.

"Like guardian, like companion," he said.

Oliver hissed as each foot hit the crystals for the first time; then he quieted. I didn't need to test him with magic to know he was in pain; I could see it in the hunch of his shoulders and the droop of his ruff. Clamping my mouth against a protest that would only offend the brave young gargoyle, I waited until Marcus and Celeste caught up before mincing deeper into the baetyl.

We ducked under a slender rose quartz crystal bar, then climbed over a carnelian crystal a few shades lighter than Oliver and so thick Marcus and I couldn't have spanned it with linked hands. Marcus kept rigid control over the glow-balls, eliminating all but two, so we moved in a tight halo of light. After ten steps, I lost sight of the entrance.

"Oliver, how's your night vision?" I asked, wishing I couldn't hear my apprehension in my voice.

Marcus shot me a sharp look, then glanced back the way we'd come. He stopped while we waited for Oliver's response.

"I don't know."

"Can you see where we came in?"

"Yes. You can't?"

I let my breath out slowly. "No. What else can you see? Are there any obvious problems?"

"The roof has caved in," Celeste said, emerging from the darkness ahead of us.

"A cave-in? Would that be enough to break a baetyl?"

She shrugged. "Maybe. It's small."

Small or not, it was a place to start. "Lead the way."

She hadn't finished turning around when gargoyles burst from the shadows. They charged from every direction and dive-bombed from above, teeth bared, claws raised, and spikes distended in attack.

I froze in shock, but Marcus spun into action, drawing his sword in a fluid motion.

"Get behind me," he ordered.

I dodged to the side to avoid being flattened by a stampeding quartz porcupine, and Marcus lurched in the opposite direction when a gargoyle dropped out of the shadows above him. His sword flashed through the air, just missing the gargoyle's canine tail.

"Wait! We're here to help," I shouted, waving my arms ineffectually.

A life-size jasper hippopotamus barreled down on me, his wide bat wings slicing through the air like blades. I jumped to the side, leaping across a broad, horizontal amethyst crystal. The hippo pivoted on thick lion legs, clawed paws shoving effortlessly against the jagged floor to follow me.

"Mika!" Oliver cried.

The hippo's jaw unhinged on a silent roar. I screamed and grabbed the elements, but they squirmed from my grasp. Frantic, I rolled under the amethyst crystal, ignoring the sharp cuts and stabs of the baetyl's crystal floor.

"Run, Oliver!"

The hippo fell upon me mouth-first, crushing me between his stone jaws.

10

I floated, a spark in pure inky onyx. I couldn't feel my body. I tried to wriggle a finger or shake my head, but there was only darkness and the rapid pounding of my pulse.

Was I dead?

Why would I be dead?

The massive stone teeth of the hippo flashed across my memory, then all the attacking gargoyles. They'd come out of nowhere, and we hadn't had a chance to fight back.

My pulse fluttered faster.

I opened my eyes.

I lay in a narrow plaster tunnel. Not just any tunnel. It was the hidden back room of the temple in New Hope where I'd rescued Oliver and his siblings from Walter's black market auction. *How did I get here?* I had been in the baetyl . . .

When I sat up, I saw Oliver. He was tiny, hardly larger than a house cat. I frowned at his small body, trying to pinpoint why my brain insisted his size was wrong. That wasn't the problem. The cage of elemental magic pinning him to the stone floor was the problem. He was trapped. And injured. His left two feet and wing tip had been burned with acid, leaving jagged patches of raw pain. Oliver's magic, his life, leaked from the wounds into the cage, strengthening it. His golden-red eyes whirled with agony, but the cage smothered his cries.

I lurched to my hands and knees, heart pounding. This was exactly how I'd found Oliver when Walter had tortured—

Walter.

Walter was in prison.

Darkness closed in on us, until all I could see was Oliver, trapped and in pain. The baby gargoyle locked eyes with me and his muzzle opened and closed in muted misery. Fingers trembling, I gathered the elements and thrust them into the first quartz anchor, countering the trap. It didn't matter how this had happened. I'd sort it out later. After I freed—

Agony pumped through my veins, cording my muscles. Magic leeched from me. I had to free . . . someone. Fear clouded my thoughts and the elements slid from my grasp. The pain abated. Oxygen filled my lungs, flavored with quartz. I sucked in another deep breath, centering my thoughts.

Myself. I had to free myself. I opened my eyes to a view warped by the elements. Magic wrapped me in a twisting cage, siphoning my life. If I struggled, the pain would return, so I held still and tried to think. I couldn't remember anything before the pain. How long had I been caged? Who was holding me?

Walter walked toward me. Once I saw him, I saw the rest of Focal Park spread around us, the dome of blue sky and puffy white clouds above me and the etched-marble penta- gram beneath me. I'd been positioned in the center and seed crystals locked the elements in place at all five points. My head went light on my shoulders. Stuck in the center, I'd be the focal point of the spell, my life drained to feed whoever controlled the pentagram. I needed to escape or I'd be killed.

I gathered magic, gritting my teeth against the rush of pain, but no matter how hard I clung to the elements, they kept slipping from my control. Walter smiled. He used brushes of air to shove the crystals holding the net closer around me, tightening the magical cage until I couldn't move.

"Good." Elsa stepped up beside Walter. The inventor looked as insane as the day she'd unleashed her gargoyle-enhancement replication invention upon Focal Park. I panted against the elemental restraints, tasting quartz in each breath.

Walter hadn't been at Focal Park, and I hadn't been alone—

Silver cracks split the air around Elsa like lines of tinsel opening into nothing but silver light.

Elsa leaned close, breathing on my face, pulling my attention back to her feverish eyes. "This will change everything."

I strained to move, but my body wouldn't respond. Elsa wove a spear of wood tempered with water and drilled into my neck. Pain like fire erupted from my throat and seared across my brain in white-hot agony. I screamed inside my head, but no sound escaped my frozen lips.

I could feel the hole in my neck.

A hole in my neck.

I should be dead. I couldn't survive a *hole* in my neck.

I wasn't made of stone . . .

Silver cracks fractured the air around the inventor as she

readied her next wood and water attack. I tried to study the fissures, but Elsa filled my vision. She plunged her barbaric elemental weave into me again. Scorching pain burned through my brain, but I clung to my last thought. It was important. *I wasn't made of stone. I wasn't made of stone.*

I wasn't a gargoyle. I could fight back.

I grabbed for the elements. Like grains of sand, they trickled through my grasping mental fist. All but earth.

I refined earth to pure quartz, and the magic solidified in my grip. Elsa loomed, another wood and water spear poised to stab me. The silver lines around her faded. My instincts demanded I defend myself. I could block her, shatter that damn magic spear before it hit my stone—

I wasn't made of stone.

The silver lines burst back into existence, and with a soundless roar, I drove the quartz into the shimmering fractures with every ounce of my strength.

Focal Park, Elsa, the trap—it all shattered. My magic hurled through the baetyl, burrowing into an amethyst cluster five feet away. The crystals shattered and reshaped, falling to the baetyl floor in perfect amethyst snowflakes.

"Mika?"

Oliver loomed in my vision, his head as large as mine, his body the appropriate size. I grabbed him and wrapped my arms around his smooth ruff. He whuffled my face with soft, relieved breaths. When I let him go, he pulled back far enough for me to see Celeste. Light fractured across the crystals around her, defining her dark outline more than illuminating her.

"She is herself?" Celeste asked Oliver.

"I am me," I said, taking comfort from the simple statement. I looked for the source of the light, surprised to see it coming from the crystals. When had they started glowing?

"What happened?" Oliver demanded. "You were fine; then you were both screaming and collapsed."

"Where's Marcus?" I sat up, hissing when the movement woke the pain in a dozen cuts on my arms and hands. Marcus lay a dozen feet away, sprawled on his back across a bushel of mint-green prasiolite crystals. His head lolled off the edge of a sturdy crystal and his hands and feet twitched, but the light underneath him left his face shadowed.

I staggered across the crystal floor to him, Oliver so close to my side that I had to grab his wings to prevent myself from being knocked down.

"Marcus." His eyes moved behind his eyelids, and he mouthed unintelligible words. I prodded his arm, and when he didn't respond, I added more force to the next poke. He twitched and moaned but didn't wake. His sword protruded from the baetyl wall a few feet away; he'd managed to wedge the tip of it between two crystals. The scabbard remained strapped to his back, but his fall had broken the rigid bamboo, and splinters of it dusted the crystals below him.

"He's trapped in the nightmare." I reached for magic— maybe a jolt to his senses would wake him—but it was as if I were in the nightmare again. The elements slid from my grasp, all but earth. Its jagged edges vibrated against my skull until I tuned it to quartz; then the element stabilized and smoothed out. Unfortunately, I couldn't do anything with quartz to wake Marcus. Growing alarmed, I lightly slapped his cheek. He swung a halfhearted punch without opening his eyes. I danced out of reach. "Marcus, wake up!"

"What nightmare?" Oliver asked.

As if his confusion summoned them, gargoyles seethed from the baetyl's geode-like walls. They swarmed over the crystals and rushed us. An enormous green aventurine bear with delicate dragonfly wings led the charge, a half ton of rock galloping on clawed feet to demolish me. I widened my stance and threw a quartz shield around Marcus, Oliver, Celeste, and myself, bracing myself for impact.

"What are you doing? Mika, what do you see?" Oliver stood on his hind legs, flaring his wings for balance, and squinted in the direction of the charging bear.

My legs trembled. If not for Marcus, I would have run, but I couldn't abandon him and I couldn't carry him.

The bear skidded to a stop just beyond my shield and reared up on her hind legs, releasing a soundless roar. I frowned. A mute gargoyle? My brain tried to make sense of it but was too distracted by her massive paws. They were larger than my head and tipped with finger-length claws; with one blow, she could kill me, yet she only waved her paws in front of her as if testing the air.

If she had been a real bear, I would have been scrambling for Marcus's sword and making as much noise as possible to drive her off. But she was a gargoyle, a reasoning creature.

"I'm here to help," I said.

She shook her head, denying my words.

"Who are you talking to?" Celeste asked. The gryphon perched on a wide tigereye crystal behind me, her sharp eyes scouring the shadowy baetyl.

"Her."

"Who?" Oliver asked, squinting at the massive gargoyle.

"You don't see her?" Frowning, I glanced to Oliver and back to the bear. She hadn't moved, and next to my gargoyle she looked . . . less. Less substantial. Weak.

"See who?"

"The bear? The other gargoyles?" Only there weren't other gargoyles now, just the bear, Oliver, and Celeste.

"I don't see anything," Oliver said.

Confusion muffled my fear, helping me pick out details I'd overlooked in my panic—like the fact that I could see the geometric shapes of the baetyl *through* the bear gargoyle. Her paws also made no sound on the crystals—none of the gargoyles' feet had. Frowning, I settled back on my heels, relaxing enough to unclench my fists, but I didn't lower the shield.

The bear dropped to all fours, nose snuffling the air around my shield; then she turned and faded from sight. Trapped air gusted from my lungs. I dropped my shield without releasing my grasp of quartz magic and rubbed my hands together, wincing when I roughed up cuts on my palms.

"It was an apparition," I said. I explained the gargoyles pouring out of the baetyl and the hippo swallowing me and sending me into a nightmare. I didn't describe the nightmare.

"I think Marcus is trapped in a nightmare, too. I got out by using quartz magic." If that was the only key to escaping the trap, Marcus wasn't going to wake from his nightmare any time soon. He was a big, bad FPD fire elemental. He had oodles of training for all kinds of dangerous situations, but he'd never think to use something as simple as quartz-tuned earth magic to escape whatever madness he was likely seeing right now.

"The baetyl must be trying to protect itself," Celeste said. "Humans aren't meant to be here. If it were whole, you wouldn't have made it this far. So it's fighting back the only way it can."

"The baetyl is sentient?" I glanced around, imagining all the crystals sprouting eyes and watching me. The thought chased a shudder down my spine.

"It is magic unto itself," Celeste said with a shrug that whispered the rock feathers of her shoulders together.

I'd had plenty of time to think about the nature of the baetyl on the way up Reaper's Ridge. I'd abandoned my earlier hope that it might resemble gargoyle magic on an immense, advanced level. A gargoyle, no matter how enraged or injured, could never create magic storms. The apparitions and nightmares only confirmed it: I was dealing with very foreign, very dangerous magic like no other I'd encountered before. Even if it wasn't sentient, it had some level of awareness—enough to tell when it had been invaded and to deploy honed defenses.

I rolled my shoulders against the urge to hunch, as if I could hide myself by making myself smaller.

"Why didn't it attack me the second time? Why did the bear walk away?"

"Maybe it recognizes you as a guardian," Oliver said.

I doubted it; otherwise it wouldn't have attacked me in the first place. If I could trust any part of an apparition, I'd say the bear gargoyle had been confused by the shield. Not many humans could manipulate the earth element through only quartz. It'd taken me years of practice to make it feel natural.

I remembered something Anya, Oliver's sister, had told me when we first met. She'd said my magic smelled like a gargoyle. Could holding a quartz shield have been enough to confuse the baetyl into thinking I might be a gargoyle?

"Do I . . . Does my magic smell like a gargoyle?" I asked, half afraid the question would offend my companions.

Oliver shrugged. "You are a guardian."

I looked askance at Celeste. She padded closer and pressed her beak to my chest, inhaling deeply.

"Your magic smells like a healer, but there are notes of a

baetyl in it." She backed away, eyeing me with fresh wonder. "My sense of smell is not good, otherwise . . . I waited so long out of fear . . ."

When I interpreted her wondrous expression, a zing of shock jolted through me. Up until this moment, she hadn't fully believed I was a guardian, but there was no mistaking the certitude in her eyes now. Celeste rolled her shoulders and fluffed her feathers, and when she settled, she looked as if someone had lifted a heavy load from her back.

Oliver saw the change in her and smiled smugly.

"Your magic is a bit like a baetyl's and it's what makes you a guardian," Oliver said. "Or maybe because you're a guardian, it's why your magic smells so good."

"Just mine? Not Marcus's?"

"Just you, Mika. Only you."

A seed of hope sprouted in my chest, nurtured by the thought that maybe, just maybe, having magic even remotely similar to the baetyl would enable me to fix it.

I took a deep breath, tasting the quartz air as I watched Marcus's hands clench into fists and feebly box at nothing. He looked helpless and vulnerable. Even his scowl was weak. No amount of prodding had stirred him, either.

"The baetyl's not going to let me help Marcus until we fix it, is it?"

Celeste shrugged. "He might be beyond help. But Rourke is not, and we are wasting time."

My stomach twisted. She was right, but it didn't make her words more palatable.

Celeste and Oliver helped me move Marcus, shifting him until he lay as flat as possible on the bed of sharp crystals. His leather pants and spelled shirt did a much better job protecting him than my clothing had. It was his head I was worried most about. I didn't have a spare piece of cloth

to put between him and the bladelike tips of the crystals, so
I removed one of his leather boots and used the leg of it to
cushion his head. He might get some cuts on his exposed
foot, since I doubted his socks were spelled, too, but it was a
fair trade-off.

I tried folding his arms over his stomach, but he flailed
and fought me, smacking his hands into the crystals around
us. I gave up and backed away, and he calmed. Blood oozed
from nicks and cuts on his hands and wrists, and I let them
bleed. If I knew more about healing people *and* could grasp
more elements than quartz, I would have healed him, but
quartz wasn't going to do him any good.

Instead, I did the only thing I could: I turned my back on
him and walked away. He'd been a true friend, helping me
when there was no incentive for him, risking his life to get
me this far, and I abandoned him.

11

From the shadows of overhanging crystals, the gargoyles swarmed, but when they drew close, they turned, parted, and let me pass. A braver person would have been able to walk confidently through the bombarding apparitions, but my steps faltered and shook, and I flinched when the gargoyles darted out of the shadows, mouths agape and faces contorted with killing rage. The baetyl might be temporarily confused by the flavor of my magic, but once it realized I wasn't a gargoyle, it'd crush me.

Behind me, Marcus wasn't as lucky. I turned, watching helplessly as the apparitions dove into his body, their ghostly forms disappearing when they touched his flesh. He thrashed and moaned, feebly slapping the air. I almost ran back to him, but I knew it would be pointless. I could stand over him and guard his body or I could fix the baetyl and save his mind.

I wasn't stupid enough to test the baetyl's crystals with so much as a grain of quartz element, but the deeper I crawled and climbed through the maze of crystals, the more heavily its magic pressed against my skin. Its jagged disharmony set my teeth on edge. A headache unfurled across my skull, the pain a dull pound compared to the sharp sting of the cuts on my arms.

I examined my wounds in the glow of an especially bright, clear crystal. Blood oozed through my shirt at my left bicep, caking the rip in the fabric. I didn't think peeling the cloth from the cut would help at this point, so I ignored the gash. A series of nicks spiraled down my forearms, with one long scratch on the underside of my right arm. Most had stopped bleeding already, and my shirt was doing a decent job soaking up the rest of the blood. My hands hurt the worst. Lacerations crisscrossed my palms, oozing blood.

Oliver and Celeste walked across the crystals without being cut, but the tension in them reminded me of their first steps. Not only was this baetyl broken, but it also wasn't their cynosure baetyl. The magic in here was not theirs, and every step hurt them in a different way. I picked up my pace.

Celeste led us to the cave-in. Amid all the flat planes and jewel tones of the crystals, the mound of soil and rocks lay like a physical insult on the otherwise pristine floor. High above us, a jagged dark patch marred the lines of the ceiling.

It wasn't a natural collapse. The sturdy beams of enormous crystals spanning the breadth of the baetyl should have prevented any part of the cavern from caving in, but if the structural integrity had been destroyed from above by the Hidden Cache miners, it wouldn't have mattered how strong the crystals inside the baetyl were.

We paused as I assessed the ugly gap in the crystals and waited for inspiration. I had hoped that when I encountered the problem, I'd see the solution. Obviously, the cave-in needed to be mended, but the scope of it worried me. Even from a hundred feet below it, the hole looked large enough to drive two trains through side by side. Enhanced by Oliver and Celeste, I could probably do it—if I had a few days *and* control of all the elements.

Which meant I needed to get started right away. For Marcus and for the dormant gargoyles waiting outside, none of whom had time to spare. Except . . .

I couldn't focus on the cave-in. I peered into the gloom of the baetyl, straining to see . . . to hear . . . something.

"What's that way?"

"The heart," Celeste said.

Yes, the heart. "Take me there."

The crystals grew denser the deeper we traveled, and their internal light increased until a dozen different shades of soft twilight lit the cavern. Celeste was forced to find her own way, not fitting through the same spaces as Oliver and me. I spent more time crawling through gaps than walking, with Oliver helping me over the larger crystals. The blood from my palms blended into his carnelian sides when he let me use him for handholds rather than the sharp edges of the quartz.

We passed two other cave-ins, both smaller than the first but not by much. I examined them without really seeing them. The baetyl's magic had grown stronger, the broken and pure notes shredding my senses like a cheese grater, disrupting my ability to concentrate on anything else.

I lost track of time. My sense of direction narrowed to the painful-sweet siren song of the heart. If I'd thought about it, I wouldn't have been able to find the exit, but leaving had lost all sense of importance. The heart was all that mattered.

I slid down the slope of a citrine crystal as wide as my shoulders and landed softly on a bed of onyx peaks, then paused in surprise. The network of crystals opened, creating a gap that stretched to the ceiling. Another twenty feet in front of me, a massive wall of interlocking crystals wove from the ceiling to the floor. I scanned the surface, hunting for an opening in what looked like an impenetrable maze of quartz.

Celeste coasted to my side from a large gap higher up, and I stepped aside to give Oliver a place to land when he slid down the crystal behind me.

"The heart is inside," Celeste said.

I'd assumed as much. "How do I get through the wall?"

"There are openings up higher," Oliver said.

"How do you know?" He'd been at my side the whole time; he hadn't had the opportunity to scout ahead to check for gaps in the wall.

"This baetyl shares similarities with mine."

I waited for him to elaborate. He ducked his head and looked away, and I realized he didn't want to say anything else. The fact that I was here, inside a baetyl, didn't make a difference. Baetyls were private, even from gargoyle guardians. Only the extreme extenuating circumstances had forced Celeste to reveal their existence, but it hadn't changed the gargoyles' instinctive secretive nature. Not even for Oliver, my stalwart companion.

"How high up?" I asked.

"The biggest should be near the top."

I tilted my head back. The ceiling here at least twelve stories high. Contemplating that height, even while standing on solid ground, made my legs weak. I pressed my fingertips into my stomach to quiet the butterflies.

In an ideal world, Celeste would have been able to carry me up and through the wall. She outweighed me by at least four hundred pounds and was larger than most mules. If she'd been a real gryphon, she wouldn't have had a problem. Gryphons and gargoyles both used air magic to fly, but the differences in *how* they did so was the speculation of scholars. All I knew was that for gargoyles to use their stone feathers to lift their solid rock bodies, they couldn't also carry anything much heavier than their own heads. Even a gargoyle as large as Celeste wouldn't be able to lift me. Her magic wouldn't support both of us.

"You'll have to climb," Celeste said.

I worried my bottom lip, eyeing the crystal wall. The smallest branch of quartz was thicker than my thigh; the largest could have fit three of my studio lofts inside. All were packed so densely at the base that I couldn't fit more than an arm through the gaps.

"To the top?" I asked.

"Not that far. You might fit through about halfway up."

I closed my eyes and swiped sweat from my forehead with trembling fingers.

"I'll go with you," Oliver said.

I gave him a tremulous smile. He knew how scared I was of heights, even if he didn't understand why.

"Thank you."

"I'll try to guide you through from the other side." Celeste walked a few paces away to give herself room to unfurl her wings, then launched into the air. She had to fly back the way we'd come first to give herself time and room to gain the necessary height. I lost her among the crystals, her dark black and purple body disappearing in the shadows. When I spotted her again, I almost mistook her for an apparitional gargoyle swooping out of the dark gap between a dumortierite crystal and a shadowy cluster of smoky quartz crystals. Her flight path should have looked erratic and cumbersome as she wove through the crystals; instead, her movements were organic. Every flap of her wings and turn of her body was timed for her to soar gracefully through the upper reaches of the baetyl.

Observing her, I saw the baetyl's design with fresh understanding: I'd been traversing the baetyl as a human, clumsy and crawling, but it had never been designed for two-legged movement. It was a place for wings and flight.

When Celeste closed in on the wall near the ceiling, she tucked her wings and plummeted into an opening not visible from where we stood. I waited to hear the sounds of her progress, but if she had to touch down, none of her foot-steps were loud enough to reach us.

I glanced back through the crystals behind us, ignoring the pull of the baetyl telling me I was facing the wrong way. Overlapping quartz of every color and size disguised the way back, hiding the cave-ins and the exit. I tried to picture how deep we were inside Reaper's Ridge. A half mile? A mile?

If Marcus were at my side, he would have already started climbing the wall and finding a way through for us. But he wasn't with me. Lost amid the crystals, he lay helpless and tortured by nightmares, dependent on me to save him.

I stopped stalling and turned back toward the wall.

"Let's see if we can find a way through."

Oliver scampered across the sharp crystals to the left and I walked the opposite direction, taking great care with my footing. When neither of us spotted any openings near the bottom, I selected an accessible-looking section near the right wall and began to climb. The crystals comprising the wall were some of the largest in the baetyl, and their girth meant not every angle was razor sharp. Unfortunately, it also meant I had fewer handholds on the slick surfaces.

Oliver had a harder time than me, lacking the traction provided by fingerprints and leather boot soles. After falling off twice, he flapped to a narrow ledge above me and guided me up the wall.

I did my best not to look down. Sweat and blood slicked my hands, and the tips and edges of crystals cut into my stomach and hips as I scaled the uneven surface. In a few places, the crystals were wide enough for me to walk along like uneven stairs, but more often, I clung to fragile toeholds and inched my way higher.

I almost cried when I reached the first opening large enough for me and looked through: Beyond the gap criss-crossed another layer of interlocking crystals too tight for me to navigate.

"How thick is this wall?" I asked, eyes closed. A tear escaped after all, but I didn't have a spare hand to brush it from my cheek.

"I don't know," Oliver said. He draped from a rose quartz crystal above me, brows furrowed with sympathy.

"Guess. More than two feet?"

"Definitely. Probably more like twenty to forty."

Another tear slid down my face. "Okay. We keep going up."

I balanced precariously on the slanted edge of an agate crystal thirty feet above the sharp baetyl floor when I finally found a promising hole large enough to wiggle through. I squirmed through on my stomach, then lay there, panting, savoring the reprieve for my tired arm muscles. When I'd regained my breath, I pushed myself to my feet and carefully stood.

Crystals jutted from every angle around me, and when I looked down, I forgot how to breathe. I stood on an aventurine crystal, and despite its almost jade color and the glow it emitted, I could see through it to the crystals below it—and the crystals below those, as if I stood on a plane of glass three stories in the air. My head went light and my heart beat its way up my throat. I crouched and closed my eyes. When vertigo tilted the crystal beneath my hands, I jerked my eyes open and stared straight ahead.

"Are you okay?" Oliver asked, peeking at me from the other side of the opening.

I nodded, my throat too dry to form words.

"The crystal is strong. You won't fall."

I nodded again and forced myself to look around. The opening wasn't a dead end—I could go up.

Lucky me.

Oliver tried to squeeze through the opening with me, but his inchworm way of walking bunched his body up too tall to fit through the gap. He shot me a worried look.

"Maybe if I fly and use my momentum to slide in," he suggested.

I shook my head, but it took me two tries to get my voice to work. "You should take a safer route. Like Celeste."

"Are you going to be okay without me?"

I thought about Marcus lying helpless near the entrance, being bombarded by the baetyl's fractured magic. I thought about the dormant gargoyles growing weaker, depending on me to save them.

"Yes." I pushed to my unsteady feet, almost grateful for the pain of my injuries to focus my thoughts. "I'll see you on the other side."

Through a beam of smoky quartz, I watched Oliver launch into the air and fly away.

———

I'D NEVER FELT SO ALONE AND FOREIGN IN MY SKIN AS I DID while inside the crystal wall. I'd worked with quartz my whole life. I'd identified as an earth elemental since grade school, but I found myself missing wood. A blade of grass, a patch of moss—any hint of growing greenery would have soothed my taut nerves. There wasn't even dust. Surrounded by all the shiny, glowing geometric planes, my flesh looked strange, too pink and rounded. I couldn't even take solace in the elements. I continued to hold quartz even though I hadn't seen a phantom gargoyle since I'd touched the wall, but the element had grown brittle and fragmented. Knowing it was a reflection of the baetyl was no comfort. I'd never had a place change the nature of the elements, and being perpetually in touch with the flawed magic screwed knots into my shoulders. Only fear of not being able to take hold of it again and being powerless against the apparitions prevented me from releasing the element.

I hurried and it still took a century. Sweat dripped down my face and stuck my shirt to my back. The cuts in my hands stung in a peripheral way until I slipped and grabbed for purchase on the slick crystals. Most of the time, I was forced to crawl, contorting myself around the overlapping branches of quartz. With the crystals so close together, I no longer feared falling to my death; instead I developed a new phobia of getting a foot or arm stuck and being trapped until I starved to death.

When I heard Oliver and Celeste, I thought it was a hallucination. I inched through a gap so tight I couldn't lift my head, moving mostly by gravity on the smooth slant with a little help from my feet. Then stone paws wrapped gently around my wrists and pulled me through.

Oliver curled around me, halting my descent with his body. I lifted my head, spotting Celeste first. She stood beside me, fitting easily on the rose quartz ledge. Gratefully, I got to all fours, then grabbed Oliver's wing when I caught sight of the drop-off beyond him.

"I've got you," Oliver said.

"Thank . . ." I forgot my own words as I took in the heart.

The wide open, perfect sphere of the heart was defined on all sides by thousands of crystals of every size, as if it were an enormous woven quartz basket—one that could fit two or three city blocks with room to spare. Hundreds of crystal ledges like the one we stood on protruded from the walls all the way around the heart, the enclosure designed to fit droves of gargoyles.

The structural beauty of the quartz sphere was surpassed only by the central crystal. It thrust from the floor nearly to the twelve-story ceiling, its girth so broad a dozen gargoyles could have stretched out on the sloped top. Unlike all the other crystals in the baetyl, which were each made of a singular type of quartz, the towering heart crystal swirled with every variety of quartz in a riot of color, the pattern never repeating.

I was so mesmerized by the beauty of the heart that when I spotted the enormous crack running through the multicolored crystal, I physically recoiled. The culprit was obvious: Another cave-in had split the ceiling directly above the crystal. I followed the length of the crystal back to the floor, spotting the pile of dirt and boulders near the base.

I didn't need to look further. I'd found the crux of the problem.

A laugh bubbled out of me. We'd made it. After months of fruitless searching and experimentation, I had a cure. I was finally going to save the dormant gargoyles.

Excitement overrode my vertigo, and I crouched to search for a way to the floor.

"There's an easy way down over here," Oliver said.

Thanks to the frequency of the protruding crystal ledges, descending was almost as simple as walking down stairs. Oliver stayed at my side, between me and the drop-off, and Celeste trailed behind us. I did my best not to notice the empty space below the see-through crystals, but I didn't take a full breath until I stood on the floor that was so densely packed with evenly sized crystals it was almost smooth.

Oliver touched down beside me, then hissed, flapping back up to a ledge.

"It hurts worse here," he said.

"I feel it, too." The hum of energy emanating from the heart crystal hammered spikes into my skull, all but drowning out the sweeter notes I'd heard earlier.

When I looked up, I spotted the eggs. Lying amid of the multicolored crystalline floor, the drab spheres struck me as insultingly ugly. There were nine, each no larger than an ostrich egg, and all were the same dead gray as the gargoyles we'd encountered on the mountain. Several were cracked open, and I looked away from the lifeless husks inside.

A flare of earth and air boiled out of the crack in the heart crystal high above me, the elements snarling together as they drifted through the crystal wall. I gaped at the newly formed magical storm. Anywhere else in the world, I would have said the spontaneous creation of wild magic was impossible. The elements existed all around us, but it was people or creatures who called them forth and put them to use. They didn't burst unguided from inert stone.

But this wasn't ordinary quartz. It might have been sedentary, but if the heart crystal could use magic to rejuvenate gargoyles and protect itself, it wielded magic as adroitly as any walking, breathing creature. Broken, it'd lost control of its own powers and the elements escaped, warped and deadly.

If saving the lives of the dormant gargoyles wasn't a worthy enough cause, stopping the formation of more wild storms would have been more than enough reason to heal the heart crystal.

I strode across the sloped floor, conscious that I moved alone. I expected my headache to get worse with each step closer, but it remained a steady, pounding pain. Still, I hesitated before touching the enormous crystal.

Without a blemish or even a seam between the different types of quartz, the smooth surface felt as soft as silk. I petted it as if it were a gargoyle, and when nothing happened, I formed a hair-thin strand of quartz element and tested the surface. My magic met the resistance of the other four elements, and I grabbed fire, water, wood, and air to balance my probe. The elements responded to me as easily as if I stood outside the baetyl. Whatever had limited my magic earlier didn't apply in the heart.

I shouldn't have been surprised to find the heart crystal's elemental chemistry to be almost identical to a gargoyle's. A little more water, a little less air, but otherwise the same—if on a much grander scale.

I widened my probe, reassured to find the crystal's elements harmonious at the base.

"Okay, Oliver. I could use a boost."

When I pushed deeper, the baetyl's magic reacted. Faster

than thought, it latched on to the line of my magic and burrowed back along the elements, flowing into me as smoothly as a gargoyle's boost.

Alarmed, I gathered myself to fight off the invasion, but the baetyl's magic was already inside me. It didn't react like a gargoyle's, either. Rather than passively enhancing the amount of magic I could use, it reversed the rules and pumped the elements into me.

I gasped when Oliver's boost opened a fresh well of potential magic inside me, and before I could utter a warning, the baetyl's magic rushed to fill the void, spilling through the link and diving into Oliver. With a pained scream, he severed his enhancement. A whiplash of displaced elements jerked from my control and shattered the baetyl's grasp. Liberated, I fell backward, landing on my butt and hands. A dozen new pinpricks pierced my palms, but I barely registered the pain above the explosion inside my head.

I stared in horrified awe at the heart, swaying in place until the agony abated to a throbbing in my temples and my blurry vision cleared. When I decided movement wouldn't induce vomiting, I gingerly rolled to my feet and tottered to Oliver's side. The gargoyle clutched his head with both front paws, his body curled tight.

Cautiously, I reached for the elements again. They responded naturally, and I breathed a soft sigh of relief as I tuned them to the proper blend and tested Oliver. Aside from a headache, which I could do little more than buffer with gauzy weaves of carnelian-tuned quartz, he was fine.

"Let's not do that again," I said, trying to inject a smidgen of levity into the moment.

"I would advise against it. This is not our baetyl," Celeste said, coasting down to land on the same crystal as Oliver.

Her wings closed over her back with a soft rustle. After almost a year of working with gargoyles, it still amazed me that their heavy quartz feathers could sound so soft.

"I shouldn't have asked," I said. It hurt Oliver just to be inside this baetyl; I should have realized asking him to open himself up to the elements here would have been a bad idea even if I couldn't have predicted the baetyl had the ability to use my connection to the elements to overpower me.

"I'm okay," Oliver said, lowering a paw from where he'd been stroking his temple. "But can you hurry?"

Despite the urgency, my footsteps lagged as I walked back to the heart crystal, and I stopped before I was close enough to touch it. The baetyl had exploited my lightest brush of magic, burrowing *into* me. I hadn't known such a thing was possible, but even prepared, I doubted I would be able to prevent its invasion the second time around. It had pushed magic into me and filled all the extra space of Oliver's boost without effort. The power it'd given me hadn't been malevolent, but it hadn't been mine, and I hadn't been able to deny it—or control it. The baetyl's magic hadn't been passive, and opening myself back up to an aggressive, semi-sentient magic terrified me. If I wasn't strong enough to seize control, the baetyl would crush me. No one would come to my rescue, either. Marcus was incapacitated; Oliver and Celeste were helpless against this baetyl.

I swallowed and shook out my arms and shoulders. For the dormant gargoyles, for Marcus, for Celeste and Oliver— for all their sakes—I had to risk it.

Marcus's accusations of throwing my life away echoed in my thoughts, and I shook my head to dispel them. He was wrong; I valued my life greatly. Even knowing the number of lives at stake, my arms shook as I raised my hands, and I couldn't uproot my feet. I didn't want to die. If there were any other option . . .

"I'm not trying to kill myself," I whispered. "I'm trying to save lives."

Before I lost my courage, I took a step and slapped my palms to the crystal's smooth surface, simultaneously sliding my magic into the heart.

The baetyl's magic bowled into me.

12

I curled my fingers against the flat surface, straining for control. The baetyl's magic battered me, swelling through my body and questing to push further, to explode through my skin and outward. I stared at my blood-splattered pink knuckles, the tendons rigid outlines. Next to the beautiful glossy surface, my blotchy skin was an atrocity.

I shook my head. The thought wasn't mine. It wasn't the baetyl's, either. The enormous geode didn't have anything so easy to comprehend as thoughts, but I could feel its *distaste*. My blood-and-sinew body was a foreign abomination that did not belong.

I'm here to help. I didn't know if I said it out loud or only thought it, but it didn't matter. The baetyl wasn't listening. It pushed magic through me, using me, and fire and water burst from my fingers, flaring up the sides of the crystal. Droplets fell back to splatter my face, but the flames roared upward until they touched the crack and splintered into a burst of sparks.

I closed my eyes and grabbed for dominance over my own magic. I felt as vulnerable as the first time I'd linked with the FPD squad in Focal Park, when I'd nearly lost myself to the overwhelming magic—only this was a hundred times worse. The baetyl's copious magic threatened to pull me into its undertow and destroy me. I fought back the only way I knew how: by grounding myself in my own individuality.

I am an earth elemental. I am a gargoyle healer. I am a gargoyle guardian, I chanted, reasserting my control bit by bit. I focused on the earth element, and the more I held, the more the baetyl quieted. When I fine-tuned it to quartz, the baetyl's magic shifted to a contained pulse inside me.

I peeled my hands from the crystal, leaving bloody prints behind. Magic sat inside me, quiet as a sleeping dragon and more powerful than twenty-five gargoyle-enhanced full-spectrum elementals. The world bounced in my vision as I pivoted to locate Oliver and Celeste. I kept my movements slow and careful, as if I balanced fine china on my head, afraid a sudden movement would wake the baetyl's magic and it'd annihilate me.

"Mika?" Oliver asked, his chiming voice high with worry.

"It's alive," I whispered, and the wonder of the realization threatened my internal balance. The baetyl's magic quivered, and I repeated my mantra, idly manipulating the quartz element without releasing it. The baetyl quieted.

"Can you fix it?" Celeste asked.

With this amount of magic, I could do anything . . . if I could maintain control.

"Whatever happens, don't open yourselves to me," I said, and waited until they both promised before turning back to the heart crystal and covering the bloody marks with my hands again. Disguising the ugly blotches helped me concentrate.

In infinitesimal increments, I drew the other four

elements to me and wove a filament to match the elements inside the heart crystal. When I pressed the blend into the crystal, the baetyl's magic stopped testing me and unfurled, as unresisting as a gargoyle's enhancement.

I took a breath and forgot to exhale. Time stilled. The serene magic held the weight of the baetyl's ancient life, and *ancient* had a texture: a velvet stillness of centuries of patience wrapped in the glassy-smooth sides of crystals that grew a few millimeters a decade. It had strength, too. Power akin to the boost of a hundred gargoyles breathed inside that vast sensation, a singular entity of immense power.

And I was linked to it.

I turned my attention up, sliding my magic through layers of tigereye and amethyst, prasiolite and carnelian, onyx and jasper and agate all wrapped in a honeycomb of elements. I lost myself in the purity of the shifting quartz varieties, and when I encountered the crack, the serrated edge splintered the velvet glass power inside me.

My breath exploded from my lungs and I sucked in another one. In my chest, my heart beat like hummingbird wings, a blur cocooned in eons, pulsing ninety times in a single minute. The baetyl's magic recoiled from the fluttering sensation, frothing inside me and threatening to spill through my skin. I gulped in another breath and held it, willing my heart to calm. If I lost control of the baetyl's power, I'd drown. Fighting was useless. I couldn't combat the strength of the baetyl; I could only work with it.

Keeping my eyes screwed shut, I nudged my magic back in line with the healthy quartz of the baetyl, then reached for the crack. I was prepared for the jagged texture this time, and I let it flow over me. As carefully as I would heal a gargoyle, I knitted the broken seams back together. The quartz reshaped beneath my magical touch, closing the base of the wound, but it didn't heal. The jangle of broken magic buffeted me, refusing to be calmed.

Pulling back to the base of the crack, I searched the enormous crystal until I found the problem. The honeycomb of elements had been shattered along with the physical quartz. I could mold the physical seams back together, but if I didn't fix the magic inside the crystal, it would tear itself apart again.

One problem at a time. Sweeping my magic up the crystal, I pulled the fragmented pieces of the quartz together and sealed the top.

My eyes snapped open in shock and I fell back from the heart crystal. The enormous pillar was wider than a house and composed of every variety of quartz possible, but I'd healed it as easily as I'd replaced Oliver's broken ruff on the train. I stumbled to the spherical wall for a better look, eyes locked on the upper reaches of the crystal. My elemental senses didn't deceive me; it was whole.

"Whoa," I breathed.

The baetyl's power pulsed inside me, waiting, ready.

On wobbly legs, I returned to the base of the heart crystal. I didn't need to touch it, but I did anyway. I needed the reminder that I had hands.

Feeding elements back into the crystal, I studied the honeycomb, slowly working my way up as I memorized the pattern, then faster as I grew more confident. The heart crystal's internal structure was incredibly intricate, but at its core, the honeycomb was gargoyle. Not *a* gargoyle, but a conglomeration of the pattern of the elements inside all gargoyles: the variances between quartz types, the shape of air element lifting their wings, the fire of life in their stone chests. All of it melded together into a complex design inside the heart—right up until the split.

Where the elements had been severed, the quartz lay dormant, no different or more magical than my seed crystals. The wrongness of that lifeless quartz stirred the ancient magic inside me. Fury not completely my own curled my fingers into fists, but the pain of my nails gouging into the cuts on my palms brought me back under control.

The baetyl's magic vibrated a warning when I grasped the tattered edge of a severed line of earth magic. I added to it as I stretched the fragile thread through an elaborate knot of fire, water, wood, and air before reconnecting it on the other side of the mended fissure. The baetyl quieted.

It approved.

After that, I worked faster. Healing the enormous multi-quartz heart crystal tested everything I'd learned as a gargoyle healer. The baetyl was alive without being a creature. It both used magic and exuded magic—and *was* magic. It was the only explanation for how the baetyl could supply me magic without weakening itself. Against all logic, I used the baetyl's own magic to heal it, and it grew stronger.

The farther up the crystal I magically mended, the more my awareness of the baetyl expanded. I could sense that the heart crystal extended as deep into the soil as it protruded, and the roots of the other crystals riddled the soil in every direction.

At the edge of my perception, I caught glimpses of a pattern in the placement of the crystals and the location of the types of quartz around the heart. I strained to comprehend the sophisticated arrangement, and the baetyl's magic slid into the open door of my curiosity, stretching inside me. I protested, a murmur of sound too round and wet. Fear fluttered weak in my chest, vibrating around the frantic pulsing beneath my ribs. When the velvet-glass power buffered me from the fear, I experienced a flicker of relief; then that, too, was soothed into calm acceptance.

By the time I finished looping and knotting the honeycomb of elements into perfect harmony, I no longer needed to use the existing edges of the torn elements as a guide. The pattern had become obvious. It was in the shape of the entire baetyl and the placement of the crystals that grew in it. It was in the location of the baetyl in the mountain. It was the essence of *new* and *always*, birth and renewal.

The flaws in the baetyl's perfection stood out as if on fire. Once the heart was healed, I dove toward the first problem. Dead baby gargoyle skeletons inside powdery eggs were not part of the grand design. I tore apart the lifeless rock and scattered the grains across the crystal-studded floor, then pulled the fine granules through a thousand tiny gaps I created between the crystals, sweeping the remains into the soil below.

The cave-in rubble went with it, pulverized and scattered into the mountain. Growing the quartz in the gap in the ceiling took time, but I accelerated the process by flinging the elemental pattern of the heart into the gap. The ridge leapt to obey my command, shaking around us. I didn't let up until crystals glittered across the ceiling, lit with the internal glow of the pattern. The crystals were small, but given another few centuries of growth, they'd match the rest. In the meantime, they completed the arc of the roof, connecting the broken magic again.

A wash of power swept through the heart, bringing pain and taking it away again. The baetyl breathed around me, more than a pattern now. I could feel the crystals in my bones, the three remaining gaps in the roof like wounds in my own flesh. I turned to examine them, only to stare, befuddled, at the wall of crystals blocking my way.

Walking took all my attention. I watched my feet lift and clop across the crystal floor, confused by the texture of my boots. When I reached the wall, I looked away from the flat brown leather with relief and pushed a hand flat against an amethyst crystal. My limb was pink and *squishy*. That wouldn't do. I pulled quartz from the amethyst and spread it across my hand, growing little crystals to coat the doughy flesh.

The quartz looked right, but it *hurt*.

Movement in the heart spun me around. Gargoyles! I reached for them but pulled my magic back before it touched their bodies. They weren't *my* gargoyles. They beat their wings, gaining altitude, then dove out of sight into the crystal wall high above me. The sinuous movement of the smaller gargoyle was familiar, but I'd never created a gargoyle in that shape.

I've never created a gargoyle at all.

I plucked at the thought, examining it. It felt important, yet it made about as much sense as the pain in my hands.

I'd figure it out after the baetyl was whole.

Facing the wall again, I shifted the crystals and walked unimpeded along the floor, bending the crystals back into place behind me without looking. Outside the heart, the remaining wounds pulsed with insistent urgency. Walking was taking too long; I unfurled my—

Where were my wings? A frantic pat down my back revealed smooth flesh and no wings. How had I become this loathsome malformation?

I quested into my body with the elements, tuning them to match the foreign liquid and meat materials. When I encountered the earth, water, and wood blend of my shoulder blades, I grafted my elements to them, converting them to quartz as I grew them.

My body spasmed, and I screamed when two blades formed beneath my skin and burst out my back. The baetyl screamed in unison, every crystal shrieking. The sound terrified me, bringing me back to myself.

I lay across a waist-high crop of variegated onyx, the sharp tips gouging into my stomach and armpit. The fingertips of my left hand hung a few inches above the baetyl floor, and I watched blood drip from my ring finger onto the prasiolite below.

Breathing hurt, but as my vision darkened, I forced myself to take sips of air. Or maybe it was the baetyl that powered my lungs. It pulsed inside me more intimately than any gargoyle's boost and sweet with possibility. I'd just moved twenty feet and untold tons of crisscrossing quartz as easily as I might push aside a gauze curtain. Stitching it back together should have taken the strength of every full spectrum in Terra Haven working all day, and I'd done it without thinking.

I'd modified my body's blood and bones and skin to grow quartz as easily as I'd reshaped the heart crystal. And it'd been easy.

I'd have grown myself wings if it hadn't hurt too much.

I whimpered when I realized I wanted to do it again. The power swelled inside me, waiting to be used, waiting for me. With the baetyl backing me, I could do anything. Fusing human and gargoyle physiology was only the start. I could level this mountain and build a new one. I could reshape the world in the design of the baetyl, making it all a perfect place for gargoyles. I could cure any disease. It wouldn't have to be only gargoyles, either. With the baetyl sitting in my head, the complexity of my own body became remarkably simple. I could be a healer of all creatures—the greatest healer who ever lived. I could perform the kind of magic people would talk about generations from now. No one would match me. I'd be more powerful than any full spectrum in the world—than *all* of them linked.

In doing so, I'd destroy the baetyl. It wasn't a gargoyle that would boost me until tired, then cut me off. The baetyl would feed me magic until it ran out.

Would that be so bad? I could cure a thousand ailments before the baetyl was tapped out. It wasn't as if this was an active baetyl. Only seven gargoyles who'd been born here remained alive. Seven lives against the hundreds, thousands, I could save. The gargoyles would approve. They'd lived out their time, and their deaths could mean something. Their deaths could help me and the world become better.

All I had to do was reach for the baetyl's magic again. It sang inside my head, offering itself. I had healed its heart. The baetyl would give me whatever I asked.

If I accepted and used all that power, I'd be no better than Walter or Elsa. Even with my head swimming with pain and addled by the baetyl's magic, I knew it was wrong to throw away the dormant gargoyles' lives in the name of using the power to save others. It was a palatable excuse to embrace the almost limitless power of the baetyl, but it wasn't morally sound. Letting the gargoyles die wasn't saving anyone. It was murder in the name of a nebulous greater good.

On the heels of that thought, my argument with Marcus flashed through my mind, followed by a zing of understanding. Marcus had been right; I'd been flinging myself into danger to save others, more than willing to sacrifice myself to save the gargoyles. With blood pooling beneath me and my body broken and weak, the irony of the timing of my epiphany wasn't lost on me.

My actions might have been noble if I'd been at all discriminating. I'd been so focused on rescuing gargoyles, I'd forgotten to treat myself with the same reverence. Worse, I'd been ignoring my own value. Just as the baetyl's power was needed here to heal the dormant gargoyles and give life to generations of new gargoyles, my life and magic was needed to heal all gargoyles, not just the ones in front of me.

I weighed my logic against my conscience. Was I being egotistical to claim my life was more valuable than any one gargoyle's? Than the lives of the seven gargoyles? The answer came quickly: Sacrificing myself to save a life or seven lives was shortsighted and foolish. I deserved better. The gargoyles deserved more of their guardian.

Just as clearly, I knew the same logic couldn't be applied to healing the baetyl. If my death was necessary to repair the baetyl, my sacrifice wouldn't be a shortsighted waste of life; I'd be saving generations of future gargoyles.

Envisioning the baetyl filled with gargoyles, healthy eggs hatching in the heart once more, I found the courage to open myself to the baetyl's magic again. It roared inside me, buffeting me with its eagerness, filling my head with its knowledge. Gritting my teeth, I severed the crystals from my back and mended my flesh. Shards of bloody quartz rained down around me, and I helped the baetyl absorb them, burying all traces of my hopeless wings. Then I rolled my fragile human body off the onyx crystals and straightened.

Oliver perched twenty feet away on a bright citrine crystal hardly larger than him but glowing twice as bright as it had before we'd entered the heart. The baetyl examined him through my eyes and gathered itself. He wasn't a gargoyle who belonged here, but together, with a few tweaks, we could make him one of ours.

It wouldn't be hard to alter him to resonate with us. The

baetyl played images through my head, showing me the process. Altering his pattern would kill him, but then we'd bring him back and he'd be better than before. And bringing him back . . .

For a breathless moment, a pattern more intricate than anything I'd yet encountered lay before my inner eye, thousands upon thousands of glowing elemental strands laid *just so* and compressed into a single spark. It was the pattern of life itself and the root of every living creature. Tears of awe dripped down my chin, and I blinked to clear my vision. To have the chance to use the baetyl's power to create *life*—

I forced myself to look away from Oliver. To make him a gargoyle of this baetyl, I'd have to kill him first, and I wasn't going to do that.

Denied, the baetyl's power receded, taking with it the knowledge of how to shape life from the elements. Gasping, I scrambled for the memory, but it slipped from my mind. I lifted my gaze back to Oliver, seeing only the gargoyle and not the elemental design of his life inside him. My chest ached, and telling myself I'd made the right decision didn't make me feel any better. I'd had *life* in my hands, and now I couldn't remember more than a fragment of the pattern.

"Don't come near me, Oliver." I didn't trust myself; if he came closer and the baetyl offered me the chance to create life again, I didn't think I could say no twice.

Swiping tears from my cheeks with shaky fingertips, I crawled over a large jasper crystal. It would have been simple enough to move the quartz out of my way using the baetyl's power, but the more I held the power, the more I wanted to use it. If I gave in just to shift crystals out of my path, it wouldn't take much to convince me I really did need wings. Or that Oliver would be better off sharing this baetyl with me. Or that the power in my hands was worth more than the lives of the gargoyles I'd come here to save.

So I climbed over and through the crystals and up the sloping floor back to Marcus, telling myself I wanted to be human and to heal the baetyl and leave. I didn't want wings or to fly. Flying was scary because it meant leaving the ground. Heights were scary.

I didn't believe any of it, and that alarmed me. I was scared of heights, but the baetyl wasn't. Fear wasn't a concept it understood.

I scrambled down the glowing side of a tigereye crystal that wouldn't reach its full potential for another three centuries and spotted Marcus. He stood, sword in hand, gaze assessing and steady, and relief made me stumble. He rushed to my side before I fully caught my balance, but he didn't reach out to steady me. Up close, I could see the worry in his lapis lazuli eyes, and behind them, I caught hints of the pattern of elements that made him, him.

"So you're scared of heights," Marcus said.

"What?" I squinted, trying to map his pattern, unexpectedly warmed by his voice.

"It's a good fear. It'll keep you safe. Fear is good." He used a soothing tone, as if he expected me to bolt.

"What are you talking about?" I demanded. The nightmares had twisted a few thread-thin strands of elements out of place inside him, making snarls.

"You've been chanting about being scared of heights," he said.

I blinked. "I have?" Damn it, I lost the snarls. I let the magic I'd kindled in my fingertips flow back into the baetyl.

"Come on, let's get out of here." Marcus gestured for me to precede him toward the exit. Blood soaked through his shirt at the shoulder. Sweat beaded and rolled down his face.

"Are you hurt? I can heal you," I offered.

"You can heal me? Since when?"

I opened my mouth and realized I couldn't explain eternity in words. It didn't even make sense to me, at least not when I tried to define it. But I could feel it in the silence in my mind and in the baetyl's strength.

"I need to finish healing the baetyl," I said instead.

"Finish?"

I turned unerringly to face the closest cave-in. Marcus inhaled sharply, and in the periphery of my vision I saw him stretch a hand toward my back, but he dropped it before he touched me.

"Mika?"

"Hang on."

"Oliver said you'd healed the heart," he said, using that soothing tone again, but I barely heard him. The quartz that had hummed inside me while I'd been in the heart grated here near the giant gaps in the roof. Magic pulsed from the heart, perfect and pure, then fractured over the broken ceiling and misshaped crystals. That had to be fixed or the discordant magic reverberating back to the heart would eventually damage it and the entire baetyl again.

"It's still flawed. Can't you hear the disharmony?" I asked, reaching for the baetyl's magic.

Marcus swung back in front of me. "You're not repairing the ceiling by yourself." The tip of his sword etched a short scratch into an aventurine crystal with his exuberant gesture. I wrapped the blade in air, yanked it from Marcus, opened a fissure in the ground, and threw the sword into the depths before I remembered embracing the baetyl's magic. Contemplating the shadowy hole barely large enough to fit the broadsword, I tried to remember the elements I'd just used, but couldn't. Had I been in control of the magic or had the baetyl? Deliberately, I stitched the floor back together, sealing the sword in the earth. The satisfaction of eliminating the threat to the crystals wasn't mine, but the fear that chased it was.

Marcus watched me with wide eyes. He'd gathered a thimbleful of elements, and I wondered what he planned to do with that paltry amount of magic.

"Are the gargoyles boosting you?"

"There are no appropriate gargoyles. She—I—refused." I blinked and looked around for the foreign, unwelcome gargoyles. There had been two in the heart.

"Oh, Mika, what did you find?" he whispered.

I refocused on Marcus, confused by the concern pinching his brow. "It's broken," I said. "I have to fix it. I have to." If he was going to stand in my way, I could send him the same direction as the sword.

"Okay. Okay, we'll fix it. That's what we came here to do. Just link with me first."

"I don't need to."

"Yes, you do."

"I'm strong enough without you." Magic trembled in my grip. It would be so easy to open the ground at his feet.

"I can see that. But you asked me to protect you. At least let me try."

I sucked in a deep breath, grounding myself in the quartz-flavored air. "Okay. Link."

Marcus thrust his pathetic amount of balanced elements toward me, and I accepted it, closing my magic around it. He groaned and fell to one knee, but he'd ceased trying to stop me, and that was all that mattered.

I strode around him to put him out of my sight. I'd

spared him because . . . because . . . I shook my head and put him out of my mind, too. He didn't matter.

We pulverized the fractured crystals beneath the broken roof and swept their remains and the rubble from the cave-ins into the mountain below the baetyl. A few layers of elements spread in the baetyl's pattern laid the groundwork for new crystals along the floor before we turned our attention to the offending holes in the roof. Unnatural tunnels bisected the mountain above, and we collapsed them all. They were the reason we'd been weakened. They were the reason all our gargoyles had died and our magic had mutated. For good measure, we grew solid beams of quartz to bisect every previous tunnel. The mountain had plenty of quartz to work with, and it was a simple matter of encouraging it to grow solid and strong.

Crystals sprouted from the gaps in the ceiling under our careful guidance, brightening the cavern with their inner glow. When the last one burst into place, healthy magic swept through the baetyl, and we listened to it chime. Every time we encountered a sour note, we adjusted the crystals, mending a crack here, smoothing erosion there. The two unwelcome gargoyles sat like ugly deformities near the exit, vibrating at the wrong elemental frequency, and we scooped them up and tossed them out.

The baetyl hummed with perfection, and contentment spiraled through us until we felt a singular entity that didn't belong. We turned to face it, scoop it up, toss it out—

It clung to us! It was inside us! Foreign magic pulsed within us, hot and unbalanced.

Panic flared, rumbling through the baetyl, setting the crystals rattling and squealing against each other.

"Mika, fight it. You're strong. Let it go."

It—*his*—voice rasped unnaturally in the hallowed air of

the baetyl. He didn't belong. He wasn't a gargoyle. There was no quartz in him, not in his magic or his body. He was a nuisance.

And yet . . .

We looked down at his hand on our arm. None of it looked right, not the thick brown-pink bands of his fingers, not our curved and doughy forearm.

"Fight it. For me."

We gathered ourselves to sever his connection with us and crush him before he poisoned our purity. Lapis lazuli eyes locked with ours and alarm spiked inside us. In me. The baetyl faltered, not comprehending. His presence was wrong. He didn't belong. But the thought of crushing the life from him repulsed me.

Fear and revulsion widened the gap between me and the baetyl, helping me find and define myself. This was Marcus, a fellow human. The man I had a crush on—another emotion the baetyl couldn't understand.

I seized upon the feelings, rolling fear and attraction in my mind to distance myself from the baetyl. I stopped trying to pull myself free of Marcus's grip and really looked at him. Sweat ran freely down his face and soaked his clothing. He was on his knees in front of me, his face pinched with pain. I frowned. I wasn't fighting him now, but he looked like he still struggled.

"Fight it," he said through clenched teeth.

The baetyl surged back through me. He was an affront to its restored perfection. He must go.

No.

I grabbed for control, but it slipped from me. The baetyl's magic roared inside me, filling my body and readying itself to bury Marcus. The amethyst crystals on the back of my hand lit up, singing in harmony with the rest of the baetyl. I belonged; he did not.

No.

I gritted my teeth. I couldn't best the baetyl's strength; nothing could. So I let it go.

It hurt. Loosening my connection with the transcendent power of the baetyl gave space for all my weaknesses: my fragile flesh split open in so many painful places; my frantic life beating away too fast; my tiny, mostly useless body gasping for oxygen in the muggy air.

Through tear-blurred eyes, I sought out Marcus, surprised to find him so close, still clinging to my arm. His features looked crude and misshapen where once I'd thought he was strikingly handsome. The crystals around us were the true beauty, so perfect and geometrical and glossy.

I caught my reflection in the side of a dark crystal. Bulbous. I was bulbous and hideous like Marcus. I didn't belong here, no matter how much I wanted it.

Aching with the loss, I shattered the amethyst crystals on my hands and reknit my flimsy, inferior flesh, then released the last pieces of the baetyl. It receded from my consciousness, its magic pulling back to the heart and the walls and the crystals all around us. I clung to the knowledge of the baetyl's pattern as long as I could, seeing it around me and in my mind's eye stretching through the mountain, so perfect and gorgeous. When it faded, I crumpled, empty and small and so very alone. Hiccuping sobs rocked my body, suffocating me, and I couldn't bring myself to care.

"Mika, we need to go," Marcus said, his voice thick.

His magic burned inside me through our link—fire, too strong; earth, too generic. After the baetyl's purity, his imperfect magic revolted me. Lashing out, I tried to sever the link between us. Elements so slender they may as well have been made of silk trickled from me. Marcus's magic clamped down around the link, locking us together and seizing control. Panicked, I jerked my arm from his, stumbling to catch my balance when my wrist snapped free. The baetyl hummed at the edge of my awareness, an invitation to link extended as soft as a gargoyle's offer of enhancement. All I had to do was open myself to the power, all that glorious power . . .

Marcus slumped to the side, eyes closed. "Fight, Mika," he mumbled, his words slurred.

Confused, I sidled closer. Did he want me to fight him? I tentatively slid my awareness down the link between us, jerking back when I encountered the knot he'd made around our link. His usually sparking, fiery signature flickered, fuzzy around the edges despite how hard he held on.

I lifted my fingers and swiped sweat from my eyes. *When had it gotten so hot?* As if waiting for me to notice, the heat grew oppressive, the air thick with humidity. I sucked in a breath, my lungs laboring to pull oxygen from the moist air. Oliver had said the baetyl should have been warmer—

Oliver!

I spun toward the exit. It was barely visible through the weave of crystals, but I remembered sweeping Oliver up and Celeste with him. I'd helped the baetyl kick them out, and we hadn't been gentle.

My body tilted and I crashed into the crystals next to Marcus. I managed to get my right forearm up to protect my head, but the impact jarred my brain, knocking my thoughts askew. When I refocused, I was staring at Marcus. He looked awful, but it was only my assessment this time, untainted by the baetyl's perception of beauty. Pain pinched his mouth into a tight line, and his eyes were sunken, the skin around them tinged with gray and the rest of him flushed an unhealthy shade of magenta. The veins in his neck stood out with strain.

"We need to leave," I croaked.

He dragged his gaze to mine, and the relief in his expression centered me. Then his eyes rolled back in his head, and he fell backward onto the sharp crystals.

13

scrambled to his side, lifting his head to feel for cuts on his scalp, cursing when sticky blood coated my fingers. Fragments of how to heal human tissue floated through my memory, utterly useless, and the more intently I tried to remember, the more the pieces slipped away. I wouldn't be able to heal him, and the closest healer was back in Terra Haven.

Oh, gods, we'd never make it.

"Wake up." I tapped Marcus's cheek. Heat weighted my already spent body, and I choked on each moist breath. I slapped him harder. "Wake up, lummox. I can't haul you out by myself."

The baetyl's magic sang to me, welcoming me back into its embrace. I wouldn't have to do it by myself. All I had to do was open myself to its tremendous power; then lifting Marcus's puny body would be no problem.

I shook my head. There was nothing puny about Marcus. That was the baetyl whispering in my thoughts. If I let it back in . . . The thought of relinquishing all that power a second time dredged a sob from my chest. I didn't think I could do it twice, and once I was reconnected with the baetyl, I couldn't guarantee it wouldn't take over and bury Marcus in the mountain.

Struggling to ignore the baetyl's siren song, I slapped Marcus, holding nothing back. His head rocked and his eyes fluttered. I leaned closer, hand raised for another strike. Sweat and tears dripped from my chin to his chest.

Marcus's eyes snapped open and he lashed out, crushing my wrist in his fist while his eyes searched mine.

"We need to move," I rasped.

He released me with a ragged breath.

It took us four tries before we both got our feet beneath us. Marcus's eyes lost their focus and he sagged against me as we stumbled toward the exit, his breathing labored. I wrapped my arm around him and did my best to support him on quivering legs.

"I'm sorry. I'm so sorry," I babbled. "You've got to hang on. A few more steps. You're too strong to give up now. I need you to stay with me. I want you to. You were right: I like you. You can't give up on me now before I have a chance to get to know you. You can't let me have blown my chance with you. Just keep going. I'm so sorry. A little farther."

We were five feet from the exit of the baetyl when Marcus toppled again, taking me down with him. Blood trickled from his nose, and I couldn't wake him. Whimpering, I pulled my leg out from under him, scraping my knee on the sharp crystal floor.

I rolled Marcus onto his back, then fell across his chest when my body gave out. With the tiny crystals packed together like so many teeth and the strangling, moist heat, I couldn't shake the illusion that we were inside a monster's mouth, waiting to be crushed. Waiting. Waiting . . .

Marcus's ragged breathing finally prompted me back

into action, and I crawled to crouch at his head, wedged my hands under his armpits, and heaved. He inched across the jagged floor. When his mangled sword sheath caught on the crystals, I used a knife from his boot to cut it free, then left both behind.

"Mika?"

I tugged Marcus another three inches and collapsed. My butt felt like it'd been beaten with a porcupine, but the pain was distant. The only thing that mattered was getting Marcus out of the baetyl.

"Is that you?"

I glanced down at Marcus. His eyes were closed but his mouth gaped open. I stared at his slack mouth, uncomprehending as the voice repeated, "Mika?"

Finally I thought to look up. Oliver hunched inside the tunnel at the edge of the crystals a few feet away, eyes so wide they looked like circles.

"Oliver!"

He flinched, and my heart fractured. I'd given him reason to fear me.

"It's okay. I'm me," I said, my voice raspy and foreign. "Are you okay? Where's Celeste?"

"It's you!" Tension lifted from his shoulders and his wings settled against his back. "Hang on." Face set in firm lines of determination, he slunk across the intervening crystal floor, whimper-growling with each step. He leaned forward as if pressing against a great wind, and I wondered what sort of pressure the baetyl pushed back against him.

Shadows danced around my vision. The heat had increased to oven temperatures while Marcus and I had climbed toward the exit, and my swollen skin ached. I grabbed Marcus's armpits again and hauled him a few more inches. Then Oliver was beside me, twisting to grip Marcus's shirt with his back paw. Together we tugged, and the large man moved a foot. I would have cheered if I had the breath.

In a few more pulls, we cleared the crystals and the ground smoothed. Oliver stopped making pained sounds. I sagged against the tunnel wall, gulping humid air.

Light from the baetyl bathed us in the cool glow of golden citrine, mint prasiolite, sunset-orange carnelian, cerulean dumortierite, and shimmering combinations of so many other crystals. I swept my gaze over the glorious shapes, memorizing the deadly beauty of the baetyl. I'd never see another again, and I'd already forgotten so much; I didn't want to forget this.

Then I turned my back on the baetyl's divine splendor, grabbed Marcus's shirt, and helped Oliver drag him up the dirt path.

———

I MADE OLIVER STOP ONCE I COULD BREATHE WITHOUT feeling like I was drowning. The baetyl pressed into me, calling to me, but its voice had changed.

I lowered myself to the ground next to Marcus, who remained alarmingly unconscious. Oliver whined, but the baetyl sang inside my head, drowning him out. Too tired to remember the reasons I had for avoiding it, too tired to resist it, I opened myself to the power, but the baetyl didn't try to link with me; it tried to talk to me.

Once I felt its magic, I felt its need. The baetyl was healed—mostly. The last gap existed at the mouth of the tunnel, where the wild magic storms had torn apart the pattern beneath the crystals. Following the baetyl's guidance, I layered elements across the opening, and when the last element settled into place, a wash of magic gusted through the tunnel, toppling me and sending Oliver rolling.

The baetyl receded from my mind, and I let it go without regret this time. I'd done it. I'd healed the baetyl. No one but a gargoyle born in those crystal-lined walls would be allowed in or out now.

I collapsed to my side in the warm tunnel, shifting so Marcus's head rested on my stomach. I needed to get him out. The humidity had decreased and the air was warm rather than stifling, but we had a ways to go. At the very least, I needed to clean his wounds and send Oliver for a healer. I needed to check Oliver, too. I needed to finish my mission and get the dormant gargoyles into the baetyl. I needed to bandage myself back together.

I cobbled together my energy—

And passed out.

———

SOMETHING BIT MY ARM, AND I JERKED AWAKE.

"Easy there," Marcus said.

I grabbed the elements before I recognized his voice, confused at the infinitesimal amount I could hold. The space was wrong, too dark and cool, and the glowballs didn't illuminate much. Where were the crystals? The baetyl—

Memory returned in a rush. I tried to sit up, but a warm hand on my shoulder held me down.

"Relax, Mika, we're all okay."

"The gargoyles?"

"Celeste says they're weak but fine."

"Celeste's okay?"

"She's fine. Oliver, too. Now hold still." He slathered a compound of kachina greenthread across my forearm, covering a dozen cuts. I hissed at the sting, then relaxed as the plant's numbing agents took the pain away. Oliver peered at me over the top of my head, smiling, and my heart eased. Marcus shooed him back, and the young gargoyle took flight across a star-speckled sky, landing a few feet away on a flat boulder. His entire body glowed as if lit from a fire within, reminding me of the crystals inside the baetyl, but it was only a trick of the firelight on his carnelian body.

I'd lifted my free arm to pet Oliver before he'd flown away, and I examined it now. Ragged fibers at my shoulder were all that remained of the shirt's sleeve, and lamb's ear bandages crisscrossed my bicep and forearm. The rest of my shirt was bunched around my chest, and the numbness of my stomach told me Marcus had already tended the cuts there. I turned my arm toward the light and stared at the back of my hand. The crystals the baetyl and I had grown into my flesh were gone. In their place was a series of six-sided scars trailing up to my wrist, the flat scar tissue lavender and sparkly like it'd caught amethyst dust inside it as it healed. I flexed my fingers, relieved when they all moved stiffly.

"Your back is similar," Marcus said. He didn't look up from my other arm, using slender strands of air to tie the lamb's ear leaves into place.

"My back?" I echoed. *My wings.*

"There was so much blood on your back, I started there, but the wounds had been sealed. It took me a while to figure out the red was part of the scars."

"What does it look like?" I wished I had a mirror or could move to feel my shoulder blades. I was lying on my back without pain, but I still wanted confirmation that I was whole.

"Like you've been run through with a sword on both shoulder blades, and the scar tissue is the color of Oliver."

Carnelian. I'd always secretly believed Oliver had the most beautiful wings of any gargoyle. I must have tried to give myself a similar pair. I heard the question in Marcus's voice, too, but I wasn't ready to try to explain the baetyl's power and the way it'd warped my thoughts.

The silence prodded my self-awareness, making me conscious of my prone position, of wearing little more than flimsy bandages and a strip of cloth across my breasts, of Marcus kneeling over me, close enough for me to count his lashes. I felt small and alone, unfamiliar with my own identity after sharing the baetyl's ancient presence, and even my body, covered in ointment and bandages and new, alien scars, was a stranger's.

I breathed through the vulnerability, focusing on Marcus's face to ground myself. He looked good, his skin golden in the firelight and his eyes alert. I wasn't surprised he'd recovered first—grateful and relieved, but not surprised.

"How are you?" I asked, hoping he didn't hear the quaver in my voice.

"Alive, thanks to you pulling me out of the baetyl." He finally met my gaze, letting me see his chagrin.

"It was the least I could do after almost killing you."

He grunted. "You've apologized enough for that already."

I flushed. How much did he remember of my frantic babbling when I'd been carrying him out?

"What happened in there?" he asked. "The gargoyles swarmed, and then . . ."

"You were stuck in your worst nightmare?"

He nodded. "When it ended, you were gone."

"The gargoyles weren't real. They were a warped version of the baetyl's last attempt to protect itself from our invasion. I escaped the nightmares by using quartz element." Talking grounded me, and my lingering sense of loneliness faded as I explained the fissures that had opened in the nightmare when I'd wielded quartz-tuned earth.

"Such a simple solution. I tried . . . a lot of other things."

"I tried to wake you," I said, seeing his haunted expression.

He shook his head. "You did the right thing. You stuck to the mission. Tell me how you ended up in control of all the baetyl's power."

"I healed the heart."

I did my best to articulate my experience, but I don't think I was successful. Describing the kinship I'd felt with the baetyl proved impossible. It'd been so natural and right at the time, but like the patterns it had shown me, the memory had faded. I settled for comparing it to being linked to an enormous gargoyle, and that seemed to satisfy Marcus.

I didn't tell him about briefly possessing the pattern of life itself. Just thinking about it, knowing I'd lost the most precious knowledge in the world, made my breath hitch with yearning, and I wouldn't be able to talk about it without crying or sounding like an idiot. Or both. I didn't have to explain the power of the baetyl to Marcus. He'd felt it through his link with me, just as he'd been in the link when I'd repaired the enormous cave-ins and collapsed all the old mine tunnels.

"It was addictive," I said. Unconsciously, I reached for my connection with the baetyl, finding only a hollow ache. Staring up at the stars, eyes unfocused, I relived the awe of holding all that power.

"Thank you," I whispered, unable to meet Marcus's eyes. "For not letting me kill myself. I would still be in there if you hadn't linked with me. You saved me from myself, just as you promised."

"Mika . . ."

I dropped my gaze to meet his. "Everything you said earlier was right. I haven't been thinking about the risks or the danger. I've been trying to do what's right, and saving gargoyle lives is *right*."

The beginnings of a scowl clouded Marcus's expression, emphasized by the flickering shadows. I almost smiled to see it, and I hurried to continue before he thought I wanted to resume our previous argument.

"But killing myself to do so isn't in the gargoyles' best interest. It's not the way to protect them. You're right; they deserve more than a martyr. They deserve a guardian who does everything possible for *every* gargoyle, the ones in front of me and the ones I can help in the future."

He blasted me with The Smile. My heart flipped and I closed my eyes. I understood his point of view, and even agreed with it, but that didn't mean it made me happy. I wanted to save every gargoyle. Letting a gargoyle die to save myself would be dreadful, and I prayed I'd never have to face that decision.

"I'm thankful you're exactly the type of person you are," Marcus said.

My eyes snapped open in surprise. He gave me a shrug.

"Not many people would have turned their back on the baetyl's power."

"It would have destroyed me if I hadn't." I would have killed him, too.

"But it didn't. You did what you came here to do. You healed a baetyl."

I smiled, and the triumph chased away my troubled thoughts. "Now we just have to get the gargoyles into it, and we'll be set."

I remembered setting the final barrier, sealing off the baetyl, and my good mood died as fast as it'd risen.

I struggled to sit up and Marcus tried to assist me without touching a bandage, which meant he was limited to guiding me up with a hand on a tiny patch of skin between my shoulder blades. My butt cheeks protested the extra weight on them, but I was pretty sure they were only bruised. Blinking, I stared at my legs. Marcus had cut away my pants, leaving me with barely enough denim to cover my hips for modesty. So many bandages crisscrossed down my legs that I resembled a freshly wrapped mummy. My boots, still on my feet, completed the ridiculous ensemble.

"How long have I been out?" I demanded. How much blood had I lost?

"Awhile. We can probably remove most of those," he said, indicating the strips of lamb's ear leaves on my legs. "Your pants did a decent job of protecting you. Better than your shirt. I still need to get these nicks on your face."

I batted his hand aside. "Have you tended your own injuries?"

"The worst of them."

"Let me see."

Marcus sat back with a huff and pulled his shirt over his head. For an embarrassing moment, my brain stopped working in the face of his broad, muscular chest and the defined lines of his abdomen. I blinked and shut my mouth and reminded myself that I was an adult and the man was injured. Dried blood caked his chest and ran down his side from a gash on his shoulder, which he'd covered with lamb's ear leaves. My brain lurched back into action when I saw the bloody tatters of the back of his shirt.

"Turn around," I croaked.

Mouth tight, Marcus shifted so I could see his back. I sucked in a breath and reached for him, stopping before I touched his flayed back. The abuse of dragging him across the sharp tips of the baetyl floor had been too much for his shirt's protective magic; the crystals had sliced through the spell and fabric, into his flesh and muscles. Blood oozed from a dozen long cuts, staining the waist of his leather pants black. It reminded me of the injuries he'd sustained during the Focal Park fiasco, only so much worse.

"Good. You got the dirt out before the cuts could become infected," I said, my voice empty. I pushed aside my horror and guilt, both of which wouldn't help Marcus. "Got any more greenthread?"

He handed me a half empty glass bottle, then rose to retrieve more lamb's ear leaves from his pack. I glanced around, taking in the campfire Marcus had built on the landing outside the tunnel opening. A few feet down the hill, the air sled lay on the ground, the dormant gargoyles scattered where they'd tumbled during the magic storms. Celeste crouched among them but she watched me, silently reminding me I hadn't finished my mission.

When Marcus sat back in front of me, I gently applied the greenthread concoction to his cuts. The compound stung before it numbed the wounds, as I knew from experience, but he never reacted. With each lamb's ear leaf I laid across the treated cuts, Marcus relaxed a little more, the subtle loosening of his muscles revealing how much the wounds had hurt. The greenthread would counter the pain and hasten the healing, but I was afraid he'd be left with scars.

We secured the lamb's ear leaves in place by wrapping him in strips cut from the remainder of his shirt rather than using bands of air. Marcus insisted, claiming the shirt was too ruined to be used for anything else.

"But air would be more gentle," I argued.

"The shirt will soak up blood. Air won't," he said, ending the discussion.

When I'd satisfied myself that the wound on the back of his head was superficial and I'd dabbed greenthread compound into his thick hair, Marcus pulled on yesterday's shirt and tenderly dabbed greenthread onto the cuts on my face.

"I'm so sorry," I said. I couldn't have gotten him out of the baetyl by any other means than dragging him, but it was my fault he'd been there in the first place. I should have insisted he wait outside. If I'd known what to expect, I would have.

He laid a blunt finger over my lips. "I knew what I was doing."

He was too close, and I felt vulnerable, covered in wounds and bandages and little else. Ignoring the tingle in my lips, I eased back. I avoided his stunning lapis lazuli eyes and the warmth they held, too discombobulated to distinguish emotion from firelight. Even dirty, bleeding, and frowning, the man was too attractive, and all my emotional barriers had been shredded inside the baetyl.

Marcus shifted back onto his heels, visibly relaxing when the move didn't hurt. "You didn't kill me. That means more to me than any apology."

"You've got low standards," I said, trying to joke.

"I saw what the baetyl did to my sword, and I knew it didn't like me or want me there."

I searched his face. "You could feel that?"

"I could feel how powerful it was, and you held it in check." His voice held a hint of awe. "Even when you looked at me like I was something disgusting caught on the sole of your shoe, you held it back."

"I didn't—" I cut myself off. I remembered thinking Marcus was repugnant and wrong. It'd been the baetyl, but it'd been me, too.

"Thank you for saving my life," Marcus said.

"I should have—"

"Just accept it, Mika."

I swallowed my protest. "I should be thanking you." If I *had* gone in alone . . . I shuddered to think of the consequences.

"You're welcome." He cocked an eyebrow at me. "See, that's how you accept gratitude."

"Ha-ha."

"Note how I'm not apologizing for blacking out and leaving you to cart my hunk of flesh out of there. In fact, you're welcome for that, too. I'm sure it made you a better person."

I threw the remaining bundle of lamb's ear leaves at him. He caught it easily. His grin tugged at my heart, and I found myself wistfully imagining him looking at me with genuine affection.

Shaking my head, I struggled to my feet. While Marcus kept his back politely turned, I pulled on yesterday's pants. Fortunately, most of the wounds on my legs were superficial and the greenthread compound had already sealed them, allowing me to remove the bulk of the lamb's ear leaves from my legs. One puncture on my right thigh and another on my left knee I kept bandaged after peeking at the wounds.

I required Marcus's help to wiggle into yesterday's shirt,

which I layered on top of my current one without removing any leaf bandages. Marcus wouldn't let me touch my shoulder blades, afraid I'd open the cuts on my arms, so I made him do it for me. He traced the outline of two hexagons larger than my palm, one on each shoulder blade. I shivered, partially in memory of the pain, partially at the feel of Marcus's rough fingertip across my sensitive skin. The patches tingled even after he lifted his hand, but I wasn't sure if it was from Marcus's touch or the scar tissue.

"Wings," I whispered, finally answering his unasked question. "All gargoyles have wings."

Marcus's eyes widened, but he said nothing, not even when I started to cry. It was just as well. I couldn't explain the jumble of emotions snarled inside of me. I mourned the loss of my connection with the baetyl as keenly as if I'd lost a parent, which made no sense. It terrified me with its impressive, unstoppable power and with how badly I wanted to possess it again. Fear had been a foreign concept for it and ultimately what had saved my life, but for a brief moment, I'd possessed the mental clarity of a truly ancient being, and I'd feared nothing. I'd known how to do the impossible because nothing was impossible. I'd been able to reshape my own body. I'd started to grow myself wings.

I swiped the tears from my cheeks and turned to the dormant gargoyles. While I walked among them and tested their health, Marcus busied himself near the fire. I appreciated the space; my emotions were too raw for me to want anything else.

In the dormant gargoyles, I caught remnants of the baetyl's magnificent pattern. It whispered at the periphery of my magic, but when I shifted my attention to focus on it, it slipped away. Sighing, I returned to the fire.

"They need to get inside the baetyl soon." They were far too weak to leave unattended much longer.

"Maybe if we can get them closer, they'll wake up." He offered me a bowl filled with a thick stew, derailing my denial; the gargoyles were no more likely to wake now than they had been in Terra Haven. They needed to be inside the baetyl to receive its benefits.

My stomach grumbled and I snatched the bowl from Marcus's hand.

"Don't expect too much," he said, indicating the food. "We used up the last of my stimulant earlier. This is trail rations, plain and tasteless, but it'll give us some strength."

I hadn't expected anything other than the jerky and dried fruit I'd stuffed in my bag. To me, the stew tasted more divine than the first-class chef's gourmet potpie.

"Got any more special tricks in your pack?" I asked. Bandages, energy drinks, real food and bowls to eat it in— the man had clearly thought this through. I, on the other hand, had brought a change of clothes, snacks, and seed crystals like I was going on a picnic where I might get dirty. Then I'd marched us into the unknown dangers of the baetyl and nearly killed us both. I was a naive idiot.

"Not unless you consider dry socks a special trick."

"I was hoping for something more like Gus's personal air sled to transport the gargoyles."

"That would be handy."

We both turned to study the toppled gargoyles. "Looks like we're doing this the hard way," I said.

"With you, what's new?"

14

W e stood in the middle of the dormant gargoyles while Marcus wove temperature-regulating spells into our clothing. It was a complex blend of fire, wood, and water, with dabs of air beading the surface. He didn't need the gargoyles' boosts, but he used it anyway; the wild magic that had escaped from the baetyl had sustained them for hours, but it wouldn't last much longer.

My eyes closed as Marcus's spell settled into my shirt, bathing me in warmth as if I stood in the sun instead of atop a chilly mountain in the middle of the night. Most of my body was numb from the greenthread compound, my stomach was full, and as my shivers abated, exhaustion crept back in, urging me to lie down and take a nap.

I snapped my eyes open. I had to keep moving.

We carefully righted all the gargoyles, linking to lift them with thick bands of air and settle them next to the tunnel's entrance. If it would have done us any good, we would have fixed the air sled and used it to carry the gargoyles again, but it was too wide to fit into the tunnel.

"Who's first?" Marcus asked.

Life flickered weakly in all the gargoyles. I wanted to insist we carry them all at once, but we didn't have the strength.

"Rourke," I said, meeting Celeste's worried gaze.

Oliver and Celeste dropped their magic into the link Marcus and I shared, filling us with power. *So little power,* I thought, remembering the enormity of the baetyl's magic.

Marcus lit the way with two medium-size glowballs, and Celeste and Oliver trailed behind us. Heat built the deeper we went, and Marcus's spell cooled my shirt in response, keeping my body at an even temperature. I tried to focus on appreciating that rather than the way my pants tightened on my bandages with each step or how my shirt stuck to the wet lamb's ear leaves wrapping my arms and stomach. Beside me, Marcus walked stiffly, his upper body mostly immobilized by the bandages.

I recognized the curve in the tunnel where I'd collapsed: I hadn't made it as far out as I'd thought when I'd been dragging Marcus.

"Mika." Oliver's chiming voice echoed in the tunnel. "I have to stop."

I twisted to look at him, then stopped fully when I saw his pain-pinched expression. Celeste had stopped a few yards behind him. "What's wrong?"

"The baetyl doesn't want us any closer."

The moment he said it, I felt the weight of the baetyl pressing against me. It didn't want any of us closer, but the pressure didn't physically hurt me.

"Celeste?" I asked.

"I can't go any farther," she said.

"Okay, go back to the surface," I said, not wanting them to wait in pain.

"Drop the boosts now, too," Marcus said.

I nodded. With Marcus and I moving in the opposite direction as the gargoyles, we'd soon be out of range of their magical enhancements. It was better to lose their boosts now than to have their extra magic jerked from us unexpectedly.

"We could wait here," Oliver suggested.

I shook my head, remembering how the baetyl had viewed Oliver and Celeste as deformed gargoyles. "We actually might be better off if the baetyl doesn't sense a connection to you in our magic," I said.

"Oh." Oliver's ruff drooped.

"Hurry," Celeste said before turning around. She withdrew her enhancement, and the level of magic in the link diminished. With a sigh, Oliver took away his boost, too, and followed Celeste. Marcus had already turned away, drawing magic through me to keep Rourke aloft. The muggy air suctioned around my feet like molasses, as if it was trying to glue my feet to the tunnel. We both leaned forward, our steps exaggerated, and I was reminded of Oliver walking as if bracing against a hurricane-strength wind when he'd returned to the baetyl to help me pull Marcus out. Several yards later, the air element grew slick in Marcus's grip, slipping and twisting under Rourke. After another four labored steps, Marcus lost control of it completely and Rourke smacked to the rock floor. I pulled magic from the link and checked his health. I didn't know if I should have been thankful or worried to find it unchanged.

"We're not close enough," I said, but Marcus already knew that through the link. He gathered air again, but it slipped away before he had enough to lift the gargoyle.

"Maybe we can drag him," I suggested.

"How much farther can you walk?"

Good question. I trudged past Marcus, and the glowball trailing me flickered and extinguished. I made it another dozen steps, each progressively more difficult. We were close, with the baetyl looming around the bend. Tentatively, I reached for it, then jerked back when a malevolent presence swiped at me. I was no longer welcome.

I turned around, steadying myself on the wall, and reached for Rourke, using the combined weight of Marcus's and my linked magic. Air slipped from my grip again and again, and I couldn't budge the gargoyle. Leaving the glowball behind, Marcus waded into the darkness with me, muscling himself two steps closer to the baetyl through brute force. The ominous weight of the baetyl tightened like a cat crouching, readying itself to pounce.

"Stop!" I gathered our magic into a quartz shield, prepared to throw all our strength into defending Marcus. He stopped, giving me an unreadable look in the dim light.

"It's not going to let us any closer, and it doesn't matter if we can't bring the gargoyles with us," I said.

He waded back to my side as if moving through waist-high mud, his exaggerated motions looking absurd in the empty tunnel. The baetyl relaxed but didn't take its awareness from us. Grudgingly, I let Marcus disband my shield and attempt to pull Rourke closer to us. Magic worked no better for him than it had for me. Together, we slogged back up the tunnel. Each step grew lighter and easier, and I fought the urge to run back to the surface, knowing it was at least partially the baetyl's compulsion.

"Now what?" Marcus asked.

"The plan hasn't changed. We need to get the gargoyles as close to the baetyl as possible. Maybe if we get enough of them together, it'll recognize them and let us take them in." It was a slim possibility, but having something to do was better than giving in to the despair ghosting my thoughts. We'd come too far to stop now.

Celeste allowed herself one mournful whine when we told her we hadn't been able to get Rourke into the baetyl; then she insisted on boosting us as far as the baetyl would allow so we didn't fatigue ourselves carrying the gargoyles into the tunnel. Oliver was more than happy to back her up.

With their help, we were able to bring the curled-up fox and the owl-headed rabbit together, but the rest of the gargoyles were too large and had to be carried individually.

"It makes my insides hurt, like it's trying to change me," Oliver said after our fifth trip into the tunnel.

I whirled to face him. "Out. *Now*," I barked, remembering the baetyl's desire to snuff out his life and breathe its own pattern into him. I hurried Oliver from the tunnel, herding Celeste with him, and refused to let them back in when Marcus and I returned to the surface.

"I need to know you're safe. Besides, there's not much else you can do. We can carry the last gargoyle by ourselves."

Oliver's defeated posture and woeful eyes squeezed my heart, but I didn't back down. He'd risked his life for me twice already today—once by entering the baetyl to begin with and again when he returned to help me pull Marcus out. I wasn't going to let him endanger himself unnecessarily now.

Marcus and I carried each gargoyle as close to the baetyl as we could, physically pushing the lighter ones closer when magic failed us, but every time we were stopped by the baetyl before we reached the entrance. Where we were forced to drop each gargoyle didn't follow a pattern; the baetyl let us carry the heavy wolf farther than the much lighter curled-up fox but not as far as owl-rabbit. The last, the sardonyx tiger, slipped from our grip just in front of Rourke.

Panting, I hobbled a few steps to the tiger's side and draped an arm over her shoulders, resting my head on her motionless side while I caught my breath. I badly wanted to sit, but I wasn't sure I'd be able to get back up.

I wondered if the gargoyles could sense the baetyl. Did they know they were mere feet from the magic they needed to revive them? I reached into the tiger with a probe of the elements—fighting to hold even a tiny bit of fire, air, water, and wood. The gargoyle felt no stronger than she had on the surface. Possibly weaker.

We needed to feed the gargoyles magic.

I straightened, seeing my horror reflected in Marcus's expression as we both came to the same realization.

"How are we going to give them magic here? I can barely hold an element," I said.

"You don't seem to have a problem with quartz-tuned earth."

True. The baetyl had a soft spot for quartz, but I couldn't do much with a singular element, and whatever I did wouldn't be enough. Feeding the gargoyles magic was a stop-gap measure until we could get them into the baetyl. If we couldn't get past the baetyl's barrier, it wouldn't matter how much magic we threw at the gargoyles; they wouldn't wake and they wouldn't get better.

Why hadn't I thought to bring the gargoyles into the baetyl before I'd sealed it? Or earlier, before I'd healed the heart? Why had I sealed the baetyl at all? I should have known it wouldn't let me, a human, back inside after it was sealed, but I'd been too exhausted to think that far ahead. Some guardian I made. I might have doomed these gargoyles in my attempt to save them.

I squelched my self-recriminations. Focusing on the past and things I couldn't change wasn't going to save the gargoyles. I needed to work with the problems as they were now.

As far as I could tell, there was only one solution.

"I need to wake them," I said.

"Can you?"

"I don't know, but I'm going to try," I said. I gave the tiger a nervous pat, wishing Oliver were at my side. The gargoyles were so weak that forcing them from their comatose state could kill them. I wouldn't even consider it if the only other option wasn't watching them fade away on the doorstep of their cynosure baetyl. I considered what I had to work with. A simple infusion of quartz magic wouldn't be enough to wake the gargoyles. I would have to attempt something far more drastic—and dangerous.

Tugging my hair behind my ear, I moved to the warthog-headed bear, the strongest of all the gargoyles. If any were going to survive waking, it'd be her.

She should have glistened like snow in the golden light of Marcus's glowball, but her white quartz body was marred with grit etched into her pockmarked sides. Sickly green prasiolite striations wrapped her wide belly and coated her folded wings.

"What's the plan?"

"First, we drop our link," I said.

Marcus didn't comply. "Why? We're stronger together."

Because being linked mucks up my individuality. Only I couldn't tell him that, or he'd guess what I planned and stop me.

"Waking the gargoyle might attract the baetyl's attention. I need one of us to be on guard," I said instead. The weight of the baetyl pressed against my thoughts, and my fear was genuine. What if it lashed out, seeing me as an enemy to its gargoyle?

"All the more reason for me to be inside the link, helping you fight off the baetyl's lure."

I shook my head. "It's not like that now. The baetyl doesn't like me anymore."

"How do you know?" The shadows cast by the flickering glowballs made his scowl more impressive, but I was immune.

"I tried to connect with it to see if it'd let me through."

"You did *what*?"

"And it slapped me aside. It's done with me."

His thick jaw muscle bounced as he ground his teeth. "That was stupid."

"Yep." No more stupid than what I was about to try, but these gargoyles deserved a chance to live, and I wouldn't stop until I'd exhausted my options—short of killing myself in the process. "So I don't need you in the link. I need you to protect us while I do my healer work and try to wake a comatose gargoyle."

My healer work, such a nice euphemistic phrase. So much better than telling him I was going to try to imprint part of my spirit into the warthog's and use my energy to wake her.

I hid my trembling hands against the gargoyle's round side. I'd shifted pieces of my spirit from my body before at Focal Park when Elsa's invention had latched on to Oliver and his siblings. It'd been the only way to simultaneously break the connection between the deadly magic and the gargoyles, and it'd been an act of desperation I hadn't realized until later could have killed me.

By comparison, using a piece of my spirit to stimulate a single gargoyle wasn't half as dangerous. For starters, it wouldn't kill me. But if I could think of any other means of compelling the gargoyles from their comas, I wouldn't have considered using my spirit. If this went wrong, a part of myself could be forever trapped inside the gargoyle, and having my spirit split would leave me mentally unbalanced or physically diminished, or both—for life.

I concentrated to keep my breathing even and not give away the frantic beat of my heart.

"We're wasting time," I said, my words clipped with tension.

Marcus stared down the tunnel, the end outlined by the faint glow of the baetyl around the corner. I knew he was weighing our options. When the link dissolved, I closed my throat around a belated protest. The magic available to me shrank, and for a second I was the small, ugly creature inside the baetyl again, letting go of all its fathomless power.

Marcus shifted closer and I purposely didn't look at him. If he read the fear in my expression, he'd try to interfere again. Closing my eyes, I grounded myself inside my body. *I am Mika Stillwater, gargoyle guardian.*

The familiar moist, earthy notes of the tunnel and the dry, smooth odor of quartz reassured me, as did Marcus's warm scent. He'd stood close enough to be accused of hovering, but having his solid presence at my back helped quiet the jangle of doubts bombarding me. The tangy odor of kachina greenthread and lamb's ear leaves wafted from us both, an unnecessary reminder of the dangers.

Fingers crossed, I gathered the familiar blend of gargoyle-tuned elements and eased my magic into the warthog without opening my eyes. Holding the magic steady, I simultaneously sank into my own body, searching for the central core of my individuality—my spirit.

I wouldn't have known what to feel for if I hadn't learned

the trick of separating my spirit and body in Focal Park. Then, the act had been a blind, last-ditch effort flowing from a string of elemental maneuvers that had already tugged me a half dozen different directions. Separating my spirit and dividing it among the gargoyles had been a natural extension of the magic I'd already been doing. Here, my actions were deliberate, my mind quiet, and loosening even a small sliver of my spirit from my body made me tremble with trepidation.

Afraid to pause and give Marcus a chance to stop me, I peeled a piece from the pulsing nebula of my spirit as easily as plucking a petal from a rose—it came free with only a mild tug. Or almost free. A slender thread spun from my body to connect with the petal, lengthening as I coaxed the petal from my body and into the warthog's. With almost magnetic attraction, the petal merged with my magic.

My breath released in a shaky hiss as the warthog's pain became my own. During the magic storms, her stubby tail and the tips of her tusks had been chipped and her folded wings were abraded. The pulsing pain of the new injuries settled into the dull aches of her body, which suffered from malnutrition and erosion. The puncture in my thigh pulsed in response, but I distanced myself from my body and did my best to ignore the gargoyle's pain, too. Once I got her into the baetyl, she'd be better.

I dove through her, searching for the spark of her life. It was nothing I could see with my eyes, but I could feel it with my magic. The essence of the warthog lay nestled among layers of elements deep in her heart. I altered my magic to match her prasiolite-striped white quartz body, then subtly tweaked the quartz to resonate more closely with the baetyl's energy.

What would have been easier than inhaling when I'd

been linked with the baetyl took my full concentration now. Since I couldn't remember the bulk of the baetyl's pattern, I had to rely on the glimpses I caught to spark my memory, then alter the delicate blend of elements to match.

I knew the moment I got it just right. The tiny remnant of the warthog hiding in her core turned, and in my mind's eye, her spirit took the form of pure golden light in the shape of her body. She stood cocooned in a sphere of white quartz crisscrossed with mint and forest-green prasiolite striations, and her liquid gold eyes regarded my spirit with profound sorrow. Loneliness from decades of isolation crashed through me, and the shock of feeling her emotion as if it were my own jarred me. Healing gargoyles gave me access to their physical sensations, not their emotional ones. The elements trembled in my grasp and I struggled to hold myself in place. Any change in my magic might push me out of her, or worse, injure her.

I'm here to help. All you have to do is wake up. I pictured the baetyl and tried to give it a joyous sensation. Hoping she could feel my emotions as clearly as I could hers, I fed her my affection, my hope for her to wake, and my eagerness for her to be whole and healthy—and with it, I twined my piece of spirit around her spark of life. The crush of loneliness cracked, allowing in such a fragile emotion I didn't recognize it at first: hope.

That's it. Wake up. Walk into the baetyl.

She turned from me, and her head lifted as if she could see the baetyl now. Her thick wings unfurled and she took a step—

Her spark blurred; then she was back in her frozen form, wings trapped against her back. Despair drowned me, and I fought to stay in place.

You can do it, I encouraged. I siphoned more of my spirit

into her, cocooning her in petals of energy. *Try again. You've only got a few feet . . .*

She looked at me, and her eyes had no room for lies. She couldn't do it. She didn't have the strength.

Together, then. We'll do it together.

Thrusting aside my fear, I abandoned my careful half-measures and yanked my spirit free of my body and into the warthog, encasing her fragile spark in the entirety of my spirit's energy. The final nuances of her body clarified in my mind's eye, and I tweaked my magic, melding with her. I turned my—our—head toward the baetyl and poured my will into the gargoyle.

15

Walk. *Take a step. Move.*

My back foot shifted, little more than a twitch, but the sensation opened a forgotten door. Awareness of my body spread upward. I lifted my head on a neck gone stiff as stone. My wings—

Fear jumbled my thoughts. The last time . . .

The baetyl . . .

I am a gargoyle guardian!

The magic slipped and shuddered in my control, threatening to fracture. I could feel my wings, glorious green prasiolite, but . . . but . . .

I do not have wings!

I yanked my magic to free it, but it snagged and held. Pain slashed me, hot and sharp. I needed to get out, to escape—

"Easy, Mika. Don't rip it. You're okay. Just take it slow."

The rumble of Marcus's voice cut through my panic and I stilled. My body shuddered with an echo of someone else's pain. The warthog. Not my body—hers. Except there was no distinction. I had wings because she had wings.

I'd hoped to use my spirit to restore the gargoyle's ability to walk; instead, I'd imprinted my spirit onto hers and it'd given *me* control over her body. Fear tingled through a confusion of arms and legs, heads and spines. I took a deep breath through two sets of lungs and oriented on the warthog's spirit again. She trembled inside my control, but with hope, not fear.

"That's better. Now ease back out," Marcus said.

I tilted my head to look at him, disoriented by the low angle. He hunched over something in his arms, talking to it, not me. With a jolt, I realized that was *me* cradled against his chest. My body lay in a loose sprawl, eyes closed, mouth open, green ointment dotting my pale face. The fiery light of the glowballs shimmered in the fan of my strawberry-blond hair and emphasized the dark purple circles under my eyes. Had I always looked so fragile?

The longer I looked at my body, the more foreign the gargoyle's felt. When vertigo skewed my sight, I turned away.

Something kissed my spirit, the feeling so sweet and pure that my heart felt like it'd sing from my chest. I stared at the glow at the end of the tunnel. *Home.* My cynosure baetyl reached for me, pulling me to it, and I welcomed the assistance.

I jerked into motion, clumsily navigating on four stiff legs. My wings flexed with each step, the unfamiliar muscles twitching in my limited control.

"Mika, no. It's too dangerous."

Everything ached, and the pain grew with each step as my body woke. My skin was chapped from tusk to tail, my feet were bruised from holding the same position for decades, and my chipped tusks stung. The baetyl vowed to soothe it all away. I gathered its siren song of promises into my heart and pushed through the pain and sluggishness of my stiff body. When I rounded the corner, the baetyl filled my vision and I ran the last stumbling steps.

A film of the baetyl's protective ward coated the opening, and when I burst through it, magic poured into me. I drank it down, savoring the cascade of relief as the baetyl massaged my body back into harmony and soothed away the aches and pains of decades.

I stretched my wings wide, body humming with pleasure. I was whole.

The elements swirled through me, and I folded them, amplifying—

That's how a boost works!

My shocked delight separated me from the gargoyle. For a moment, I was an amazed observer. I'd never understood how a gargoyle could create more magic out of the existing elements, but from my new perspective, it seemed obvious. Then my access to the world through her eyes slipped from my control. The space between our spirits grew, and I had the impression of the warthog regarding me with the wise eyes of her spirit before she shoved me from her body.

I tried to hang on, clinging to elemental fibers inside her until I saw the damage I created. I wasn't supposed to hurt gargoyles. I was a healer.

With that thought, I lost my anchor and my detached spirit shot fast as an arrow back to my body, slamming home.

I gasped for air like I'd been underwater, back arching, eyes flying open to stare up at the shadowy ceiling of the tunnel. My heart hammered in my chest and I panted, trying to remember who I was, where I was, *what* I was.

I am Mika Stillwater. I am a gargoyle healer. I am a gargoyle guardian.

My spirit settled into my body, binding with the minute

piece I'd left behind. I couldn't see it in myself as I could in the gargoyle, but I didn't need to. I could feel the rightness. I wriggled my fingers and toes, stifling a groan as my body's pains awoke. The blissful sensation of the baetyl healing the warthog's wounds faded to a wistful memory.

I sat up, and Marcus's hand settled at my back to support me. I braced a hand on the floor to balance against a wave of dizziness while I looked around. It hadn't been a dream. The warthog was gone.

"I did it." I grinned at Marcus. "I got a gargoyle into the baetyl." I'd walked her body in as if it were my own. The thought made me queasy and giddy at the same time. "If I can do it once, I can do it seven times. I'm saving all these gargoyles' lives!"

"I thought you were done with shoving your life in front of every problem."

"I am."

"Then what do you call that stunt?"

"A calculated risk that—"

"Risk?! This is exactly what you did at Focal Park."

"No, it's not. I've thought this through—"

"You shoved your spirit into a gargoyle just like last ti—"

"I didn't divide myself up."

"Oh, so that makes it better?" Marcus rose to his feet in a smooth motion and paced away from me, fists clenched.

"Listen to me. I'm giving the gargoyles the strength they need. I can't get them into the baetyl by physical or magical strength, but I can by—"

"By sticking the essence that makes you, you into another living creature. That's not *right*. It's not natural or safe or a reasonable risk."

"It is for me."

I'd come here with the impossible mission of battling

my way through deadly magic storms, finding a secretive baetyl hidden inside the mountain, fixing it without even knowing exactly what a baetyl was, and then getting the sick gargoyles inside. I had doubted the success of this mission a thousand times. Yet, despite all the hardships, I'd done it. I couldn't—*wouldn't*—stop this close to the finish line.

"I'm not attempting this with just any troubled creature. I'm a—"

"Don't say it."

"Gargoyle guardian," I finished.

"Damn it."

"Whatever it is that made me capable of healing the baetyl is the same part of me that makes it okay for me to transplant my spirit into a gargoyle. *Temporarily.* My magic is somehow close to theirs. It means they're safe with me and I'm safe with them. This isn't a martyr mission."

Veins stood out on Marcus's neck as he loomed over me, his forearms corded with tension. "You didn't know who you were."

"I was disoriented for a moment."

"You were unresponsive for fifteen minutes."

"That long?" I rolled to my knees— Wait, hadn't I been standing in front of the warthog? I recalled a shadowy memory of looking at myself through the warthog's eyes. Marcus had been holding me in his arms. "Ah, thank you for catching me?"

Marcus gave me an exasperated look. "Someone had to protect the tunnel from the impact of your thick skull."

"Good point. I'll make sure to be sitting next time." Fifteen minutes? I assessed the flickers of life inside the remaining gargoyles. I'd have to leave the strongest for last and work faster. None of the gargoyles looked like they would survive another hour.

"Are you sure there's no other way?" Marcus asked.

I stood but relaxed my defiant posture when I saw his concern.

"I can't think of one. Can you?"

He shook his head.

Rourke's will to live was fading fast, and I surged to his side, sat, and shoved a braid of magic and spirit into him. Marcus cursed, then his warmth settled beside me.

"Damn it, be careful," he growled.

I was faster this time, dropping through the layers of Rourke's pain and tweaking my magic to resonate with his unique signature. The baetyl's pattern drifted in and out of my awareness, and I altered my magic to harmonize with it when I could but didn't let myself be distracted by chasing it.

When my magic clicked in perfect synchronization with Rourke, I saw him in my mind's eye. He didn't react, his inner self as frozen as his physical body. Gently, I wrapped him in love and admiration and thick layers of my spirit. We merged, and the weight of his body became my own.

I knew what to expect this time, but it made it no less disorienting. Or easier. I gathered my will and funneled it through my spirit and out to our limbs. Forcing our body to fold so we could walk on all fours took herculean effort. Our wings hung heavy and useless at our sides, trailing on the rock ground for four torturous steps before the baetyl's song infiltrated my body. After that, each step grew easier. I still had to shove and strain to carry my unwieldy bulk, but the song urged me on.

Crossing into the baetyl felt like walking through a cleansing shower. I closed my eyes in bliss as magic bathed me from the inside out and the outside in. After decades of fighting, I relaxed and reveled in being alive. When I opened my eyes, I saw the warthog take flight, flapping lazily to a higher perch, folding and twisting the baetyl's magic for the sheer joy of it.

I rolled onto my back and spread my wings on the tiny crystals, their sharp points a delightful massage against muscles and feathers long unused. My antlers scraped the crystals, making the quartz sing.

Something nudged me, a gentle but persistent prod, and I spiraled down into my—our—body. Blinking, I looked up into the bright eyes of Rourke's spirit. His gratitude wrapped me like a soft blanket even as he used an antler to push me again. With a smile, I let go, and my spirit winged back to my human body.

"Mika?"

Who?

I squinted, the bright light hurting my eyes. Someone crouched over me. *Marcus.*

"I am Mika Stillwater," I said, and the words felt right even if I wasn't completely sure what they meant.

"You are a gargoyle healer and guardian."

Right. My spirit and mind clicked into sync. I was in Marcus's lap, cradled against his chest and arm. *Safe,* my heart whispered.

Seeing the empty tunnel where Rourke had stood minutes before made my heart swell with elation. I couldn't wait to deliver the good news to Celeste. We'd done it: We'd saved her mate.

"How long?" I asked.

Marcus shook his head. "I don't know. A little longer, I think."

Longer? I'd tried to be faster, but it had been hard to remember my purpose over the call of the baetyl. If Rourke hadn't nudged me from his body, I'd still be there.

Marcus studied my face, worry lines etching his forehead. He held me close enough that I could count the flecks of navy in his lapis lazuli eyes, but I looked away, not wanting him to see how much I didn't want to move.

Pushing out of his arms took willpower I didn't have to spare, and I selected the next weakest gargoyle—the rabbit-owl. Like Celeste, whose head and front legs were those of an eagle, his front legs and chest were all owl, and though his body was far more compact than the two previous gargoyles I'd inhabited, once I wrapped him in my spirit, it took just as much effort if not more to hop him into the baetyl. Despite my best intentions, I forgot about everything but the baetyl's song and the glorious sensation of being home until the gargoyle raked his talons against my spirit and forced me back to my body.

Marcus was holding me when I opened my eyes to the bleak brown walls of the tunnel, and he assured me I was Mika Stillwater, gargoyle healer and guardian. I watched his lips move, heard the words vibrate against my eardrums, but he had to repeat himself several times before the sounds connected with my brain and made sense.

The citrine and smoky quartz badger with a seahorse head was next, then the onyx wolf. Following my magic into the gargoyles to find their weak spirits was easier when I started with my body right next to theirs, and if Marcus hadn't been watching, I would have crawled to the gargoyles. Instead, I forced myself to stand and walk, though Marcus had to wrap an arm around my waist to keep me from falling. He didn't comment on my fatigue or argue for me to slow down. The gargoyles were fading too fast for me to take a break. Or a nap.

I dearly wanted a nap—at least when I inhabited my own body. When I was in the baetyl, in those timeless moments before the gargoyles kicked me out of their bodies, I lived in their sublime bliss. There, I was rejuvenated. The baetyl, which had been a deadly, alluring source of power to me when I'd climbed into the heart and healed it, was sweet and comforting when I forgot I wasn't a gargoyle. It made snapping back to my own body worse each time, the euphoric moments in the baetyl emphasizing my body's growing misery. Sweat and time counteracted the green-thread's numbing properties, and a multitude of injuries clamored with increasing fervor each time I settled back into my own skin.

Worse was the loss of the baetyl—its beauty, its soothing song, its promise of rejuvenation.

I lingered in the badger and longer still in the wolf, forgetting myself in their all-consuming relief to be home and healing. With each gargoyle, I gained more under-standing of how they interacted with magic, and it was amazing. As a human, I could use the elements, channeling them into different shapes and patterns to create an outcome. As a gargoyle, I didn't have to reach for the elements; they saturated me. Amplifying magic was a simple matter of folding it to make the elements denser. Focusing the effect, I could direct it where I wanted . . .

Each time I came back to my body, what had been so clear as a gargoyle didn't make sense as a human. How could the elements be folded? How could you direct magic without using it? I tried to cling to the memory, but the drone of a voice would cut through my puzzled thoughts, and I'd lose it.

"You are Mika Stillwater, gargoyle guardian and healer."

I focused on the intense stare of the man above me and the words he delivered with a vehemence that said they were important. "Your parents are water elementals. You live in Terra Haven."

I frowned at the unfamiliar syllables.

"Say it with me. Say, 'I am Mika Stillwater.'"

My hip throbbed, my arms stung. My head wanted to fall off my shoulders. Nothing was proportioned right. Where were my wings?

The man jabbed my breastbone with a stiff finger. I winced and frowned at him. A glowball hovered close beside us, casting stark shadows that pooled in the crease between his eyebrows and the hollows around his eyes.

"You. Open your mouth and say it," he ordered.

"I am Mika Still . . ."

"Mika Stillwater. Say it."

"Mika Stillwater." I repeated the words twice, their shape familiar in my mouth.

"You are the foolish and stubborn gargoyle guardian, Mika Stillwater."

I stiffened, recognizing my name. Alarm skittered down my spine as I reconnected with my body. I hadn't recognized myself. At all.

Marcus must have read the fear in my eyes and known I'd returned, because he stopped talking. He shifted, pulling me tighter against him.

"You're okay. You're back. Everything's okay."

Everything was not okay. My hands didn't lift when I reach for Marcus. The baetyl sang just below my hearing range, a hum that made my jaw ache and sparkles dance through my vision. I didn't want to be able to hear it—it was calling to gargoyles, and I *shouldn't* be able to hear it—but I couldn't stop myself from straining to make out the notes. The harder I concentrated, the more my head pounded. But that wasn't the worst of it. Without looking, without moving, I could feel the remaining tiger and fox gargoyles.

My awareness of the gargoyles wasn't natural. It wasn't human. It was something the baetyl could do. I should have needed magic, but I'd blurred the lines. I'd reshaped myself too many times and too quickly, first in the baetyl and now with the gargoyles. I was losing myself.

When I shifted, the tunnel darkened and spun. I righted it with a blink. "How long?"

"Too long."

"Okay. Tiger next." Just as I could sense the location of both gargoyles, I didn't need magic to tell she was the weaker of the two.

"Mika . . ."

"She's fading too fast."

"So are you."

I tilted my face up to look at Marcus, my head resting on his shoulder, my body cradled by his. I fought the desire to close my eyes and relax against him. "I'll recover."

"Take a break," he urged.

I tried to stand, but my body didn't even sit up. I couldn't feel my feet. Dropping my lashes to hide my panic, I focused on wriggling my toes. When they responded, I let out a slow breath. *Tired. I'm just tired.* If I stopped now, I wouldn't be able to start again, not for hours. By then, both gargoyles would be dead and I would never be able to live with myself.

The tiger stood frozen at the bend in the tunnel behind us, farther from the baetyl entrance than the fox. She was only five feet from us, but it might as well have been five miles if I had to walk it alone.

"Please don't try to stop me."

Marcus scowled, but he surprised me when he stood with me in his arms and walked to the tiger.

"Thank you."

I fell into the tiger and didn't stop falling until I stood in front of her inner self. Her body's shape ghosted at the edges, as if the golden light of her spirit were evaporating.

Or dying.

I saw the truth of my realization in her eyes and felt her acceptance of her death pulse between us.

No. I'm here to save you. The baetyl is right here. *All we have to do is walk a few dozen feet.*

I pushed my spirit closer, but she flared bright. The impression of a roaring tiger, sharp teeth, and rending claws flashed almost too fast to follow. I retreated, and the gargoyle's fuzzy shape returned.

You can't give up, I commanded, not sure how much she could hear. I willed her to live, to fight. She smiled, her cat mouth curling up around her thick muzzle, and sent me a feeling of serenity.

Don't you dare. I shoved my spirit toward her again, enveloping her, holding the effervescent pieces of her together by sheer will. She didn't struggle this time; she purred. The soundless vibrations resonated with love and gratitude . . . and forgiveness.

I clung to her, desperate to save her. We were so close. If she would hang on just a bit longer, I could save her.

I poured more of my will into hers, capturing her, holding her. I could do this. I could walk her into the baetyl.

My awareness expanded to her limbs—

Sharp pains tore through me. It wasn't the gargoyle fighting; she'd relaxed in my grasp. It was the strain of anchoring the gargoyle to her body eating through me, pulling my spirit apart. It shredded my strength, shredded me. If I held on much longer, she would pull me apart.

If I let go, she'd die.

I hung suspended in that moment of love and guilt, forgiveness and torture. I couldn't save her. I couldn't abandon her.

I couldn't abandon the fox, either. If I clung tight enough, fought hard enough, I could overpower the tiger's fading will and walk her into the baetyl, but doing so would leave nothing of me to help the fox.

It'd leave nothing of *me*. If I saved her, it would be the last thing I'd do, and I'd promised myself I would be more than a martyr. I'd be a true guardian.

Letting go hurt far worse than holding on. I released the tiger, and in the agony of my decision, her gratitude caressed like a soothing balm across my spirit. She turned her golden tiger's head to me, and her eyes held nothing but love.

Then her form shifted and stretched, growing less and less substantial. I waited beside her, sending her my love, until a wash of profound relief exploded from her spirit, bowling me over. When I reoriented, she'd ceased to exist.

My eyes opened on a blurry world. Tears ran down my temples into my hair, and the sounds escaping my throat and echoing in the tunnel frightened me.

"Mika?"

"She didn't make it," I sobbed. I couldn't find my paw—hand—to wipe away the tears.

The baetyl's song filtered through my tears, new mournful notes quieting my sniffles. I cocked my head, listening. I was really hearing it, the melody unfurling inside me.

"I'm so sorry, Mika."

Power swelled behind that song, urging me back to my task. I had one more gargoyle to save, and the fox's life guttered on the cusp of being extinguished.

"I need to help the fox," I mumbled through numb lips.

"No. You need to rest. You can't—"

I glanced up into his eyes, and I knew the weight of the baetyl looked out at him through mine.

"Mika . . . don't—"

"I'm coming back," I whispered, and I didn't know if I was talking to Marcus or the baetyl.

"Mika!"

I dropped out of my body into the fox's, and it felt like going home.

16

I uncurled my tail, surged to my feet with an assisting flap of my long wings, and stretched. My awareness of my body puzzled me. Of course my legs were all proportional and used for walking. Of course I had wings. Of course my body was beautiful tigereye and citrine.

Every square inch of me hurt, my body cramped from decades of paralysis and my skin gouged and chapped. The itch in my tail was new. I twisted to examine the patch of clear quartz sealing a fresh wound and caught sight of the humans. The man knelt over a sleeping woman, his face close to her ear, his lips moving. His voice buzzed against my mind, and I shook my head to dispel a wave of dizziness. I focused on my tail again, puzzling over the anomalous patch. It looked like the work of a healer, but I didn't remember a healer. I didn't remember being hurt. I didn't remember . . .

My baetyl's song whispered in my ears, chasing every other thought from my head. I stretched the stiffness from my paws again, then trotted down the tunnel. Home. I was going home after far too long.

I burst into the baetyl and leapt into flight. Magic breathed through me, and I hungrily folded it into myself. My wings beat, tenderly at first, then with greater ease. I soared through the baetyl, letting the air carry my pain away. I was whole.

My wings banked, the muscles acting as if they had a mind of their own, and I stumbled to a landing on a high grotto filled with rose quartz. Shaking my head, I turned around and prepared to leap, but my back legs refused to budge.

I growled, the sound ragged in my unused throat. I wouldn't be frozen again. I was safe. I was home. Nothing could stop me.

I pushed from the ledge and my heart lodged in my throat when my wings didn't open. Clawing at the air, I caught the edge of a thick amethyst crystal, nails scraping the slick surface before my wings finally flared open and I shoved into the air. I'd barely gained altitude when my body dove out of control, pulling up just before I crashed into the jagged floor.

Whining, I tried to look at my wings, now folded on my back, but I couldn't move my head. Panic thundered in my heart. I fought the hidden bonds as the baetyl darkened until I couldn't see.

The fox split her spirit from mine. The shock of separation sliced through me like a blade. Distressed, I rushed the fox.

Don't do this. I need you, I thought. She could remain in the baetyl, in our home. With her, I was safe. She was alive. She wouldn't die. I'd never have to leave.

The fox nipped me, and her spirit's sharp teeth pinched. I didn't care, too filled with the terror of being abandoned. I swelled, wrapping around the fox again, trying to join with her, but she wasn't compliant this time. She fought back, and her nips became agonizing bites and unheard growls. Flinching, I gave ground and she chased me until I had nowhere left to go.

I popped free of the fox's body and floundered in an abyss. All sense of direction and purpose drifted away from me. I hung there, suspended in nothing, lost and confused.

"Go home, Guardian," someone growled.

Home? I spun the word in my thoughts, then released it into the void. It divided and multiplied, taking a thousand different shapes until . . .

Home. This was home. It was in the shape of every layer of quartz and in the interaction of every element. And the elements . . . They floated with me, crisper than I'd ever seen them, five pieces of the same magic. Enraptured, I drifted among them, glorifying in their perfection. The pattern of the baetyl filled me with rapture; the patterns of life moving in it elicited pride and awe. I belonged here, a part of this world and the elements. I couldn't see myself, but I could feel *me*. I was beautiful and perfect, in harmony with everything around me.

Fire lit through me, the scorching pain spinning the world around me. A buzzing enveloped me, and I pushed it away, only to be singed again. I screamed and tried to fight off the flames, but they'd disappeared. Unbalanced and hurting, I sought out my previous bliss, but it eluded me. The clarity of the elements had blurred, disguising the gorgeous patterns hidden among them. Something had stolen my perfection, and without it, I didn't belong here.

Irate, I chased the fire the next time it attacked. When I found the source, I pounced, wrapping around it to extinguish it. Flames licked through me. Snarled inside the agonizing blast were the other four elements in a pattern I didn't recognize and that didn't matter. It wasn't a true pattern. It wasn't beautiful. It was a trap.

I fought, entangling myself further. The buzzing had become a drone that encased me, constricting the binding elements.

"Damn it, Mika, I won't let you die."

Agony seared through me and my eyes burst open. A claustrophobic world greeted me, filled with dreary shades of brown and black. I closed my eyes. I wanted to go back to floating with the elements.

Fresh pain forced my eyes open again.

"You are Mika Stillwater. You are a gargoyle healer and guardian. You . . ."

The sounds washed over me. My eyes roved over the tiny, drab world, stopping when they encountered blue. It wasn't gargoyle blue but it had its own beauty, flecked with navy . . .

The baetyl's sweet promise sang at the edge of my perception, and I closed my eyes again and stretched for it. I started to drift free of the trap, but sparks rained pain through me, tightening me in place. When the world jostled, I looked around with fresh hope, but I hadn't escaped. Above me, the rocky brown ceiling shifted and the baetyl grew farther away, its song fading. Tears leaked from my eyes.

"Your parents are water elementals. You have a younger sister. You once seared your eyebrows off in an Elemental's Apprentice duel. You make miniature figurines with quartz that look like they could come alive."

Golden warmth hit my face and I squinted against the bright light. A vast indigo sky arched overhead and spun toward a lighter blue horizon and the sun's fiery orb cresting the green tree-covered hills. Wind picked at my loose hair, carrying the crisp scent of dew and pine and damp soil. The man was still speaking, his voice a pleasant rumble. I relaxed and let myself go.

The trap holding me loosened and I was floating. All remnants of pain faded, taking with it my exhaustion. I didn't have to fight anymore. I could just let go.

White light swept over the hills, erasing them. It grew brighter until it consumed the sky, my body, and everything in between. I looked into the face of every possibility, every truth, and love infused me. Everything was okay. All I had to do was ...

Let ...

Go.

17

"**M**ika!"

The trilling voice speared through me. The bright light trembled.

"Mika, wake up."

Oliver.

I fell, sinking into a body. *My body?* Air rushed into my lungs, drawing pain in its wake. Groaning, I opened my eyes.

A carnelian gargoyle stood over me, the sunlight on his flared wings making them look like fans of flame. He thrust his worried square face into mine. "Mika?"

Oliver. I knew him, knew he was important to me, but everything felt fuzzy. The gargoyles—

I had to get the gargoyles into the baetyl!

Tentatively, I gathered elements to reach for Oliver. He couldn't move himself, so I had to get him inside before he died. Except, he *was* moving. I let the elements unravel, confused.

"Come on, Mika. Come back to us, you stubborn woman."

I shifted to look for the source of the rough, masculine

voice, surprised to find the man's face inches from mine. I was in his arms, and the feeling was as familiar as his voice. *Marcus.* His fierce scowl should have been intimidating, but it infused me with warmth.

"You are Mika Stillwater. You live in Terra Haven in a tiny apartment in Ms. Zuberrie's house. Your best friend is Kylie Grayson. Oliver is your gargoyle companion."

A zing of recognition sparked. He was telling me about myself. I tried to concentrate but the words couldn't compete with my emotions. I liked being held by Marcus. I liked the concern so evident in his tone.

Oliver rested his muzzle on my stomach, and a rush of love for the gargoyle drowned out all other sensations. When I turned back to Marcus, an echo of that love, softer, less sure, darted through me. Lifting a hand to grip the back of his neck, I pulled Marcus to me.

The soft heat of his surprised exhale fanned across my mouth, followed by the delicious, shocking contact of his lips. Tingles raced through my body and my spirit snicked home.

Marcus hesitated; then he kissed me back, his arms tightening around me.

"I am Mika Stillwater," I said when he pulled back a few inches.

His luminous blue eyes searched my face and a decade of worry lifted from his expression.

"Thank you for saving me," I said.

"I thought you were going to die," he whispered, the words a confession.

"I think I did." With every passing second in my body, my memory of my spirit being adrift faded, but the emotional resonance remained. I'd experienced an unearthly bliss born of an indescribable harmony, and the sensation remained imprinted on my spirit.

"But you brought me back. You and Oliver."

Oliver whined and Marcus helped me sit up so I could hug the young gargoyle. He cradled me gently in his stone wings, his silent enhancement a balm to my battered spirit. The knowledge of how to fold the elements like a gargoyle lurked on the edge of my memory but refused to surface. Snippets of the baetyl's pattern and the pattern of all life taunted my memory, too, but I didn't chase them. That wisdom wasn't meant for me, not now. Not in this life.

I rolled the elements, savoring their textures while I petted Oliver's smooth scales. I could feel him in the boost almost like a magic signature. My awareness of Oliver wasn't new; I'd been able to distinguish his enhancement from other gargoyles' for a while now.

The same couldn't be said for my newfound ability to pinpoint the location of him, Celeste, and, much fainter, the gargoyles in the baetyl, without looking. I didn't know what to make of it, but I'd have plenty of time to think about it. Later.

When Oliver released me to snuggle against my side, I sought out Celeste with my eyes. She perched above the cave opening, giving us space.

"Rourke is safe," I said. The last word caught in an unexpectedly thick throat as I remembered the tiger fading in front of me. Despite my best efforts, she'd died on the doorstep of her baetyl. Her profound relief at the end didn't assuage my guilt completely, but I thought I understood it. I still wished I could have saved her.

"Your bravery will never be forgotten, Guardian Mika," Celeste said.

I blinked away my tears and acknowledged my success.

I'd done it. I'd saved the dormant gargoyles and healed a baetyl. I'd earned the title the gargoyles had bestowed upon me.

"My name is Mika Stillwater. I am a gargoyle guardian," I whispered, feeling the truth of my words resonate through my spirit. Joy sang in my veins when I turned to Marcus. "And I want to get busy living."

I leaned toward him and he met me halfway, a smile on his lips when we kissed.

EPILOGUE

The baetyl chased us off Reaper's Ridge. By the time Marcus had repaired the sled, its malevolent, squeezing pressure had inflicted us both with splitting headaches. Jittery with a need to leave, I stumbled to collect our gear and shooed Oliver into the air to meet us down the mountain where it was safer. Celeste stayed only because she had to pull the sled, and she huddled in a tight knot, pain pinching her face. Marcus settled the loop of rope around Celeste's chest as I was crawling into the back of the hovering sled, and she set off, shoulders hunched, the moment he joined me.

In terse silence, Marcus twined his fingers through mine, and we clutched the sides of the sled for balance with our free hands as Celeste galloped down the jagged slope, following the path of least resistance. I twisted to watch the tunnel entrance disappear, jaw clenched against the escalating pain hammering against the inside of my skull.

When a fold in the hillside hid the opening from view, my breath hitched with unexpected grief. I would never see the baetyl again—never again be a part of its awesome, terrifying power. Tears blurred my vision as I glanced down to my hand intertwined with Marcus's. I wasn't the same woman who had climbed Reaper's Ridge. The sparkling amethyst scars in my pale flesh and the twin carnelian hexagons on my shoulder blades were my only visible souvenirs, but the baetyl had wrought changes in me that went far deeper. For a few brief moments, I'd been so much more than a singular person in a tiny, fragile body. I'd been linked with a truly ancient entity, privy to spectacular secrets beyond the scope of human understanding.

I mourned the loss of that connection far more than the loss of the baetyl's power.

Marcus squeezed my hand. "Are you okay?" he shouted, the wind whipping his words away.

I nodded because it was easier than trying to explain, especially while being jounced around the back of the sled during our breakneck descent.

The faster Celeste ran, the tighter my fear ratcheted. I checked over my shoulder repeatedly, every time expecting to spot a ravenous monster barreling down on us. It was only the irrationality of my growing panic that helped me see it for what it really was: another of the baetyl's natural defenses awakening. Knowing my escalating terror was generated by the baetyl did nothing to calm me. I'd been a part of its immense power—playing off my unconscious fears was the least of what it could do.

Marcus released my hand to pull his crossbow from his bag and lay it across his lap. He scanned our surroundings for the enemy his brain insisted lurked just out of sight.

"It's not real. It's the baetyl."

"I know, but this helps," he said, and I realized he hadn't notched an arrow.

Gradually, the agony in my temples subsided, along with

the hunted feeling that had lodged between my shoulder blades. Celeste slowed to a less hazardous speed, but she didn't stop to rest. Lulled by her steady footsteps and the cessation of pain, I closed my eyes, jolting awake when my body tilted.

"Why don't you lie down?" Marcus suggested.

He scooted to the front of the sled to sit sideways behind the driver's box, one arm draped over the seat so he could lean against it. Until a healer could mend the lacerations on his back, resting against his side was probably the most comfortable position he could attain. I stretched out with my head pillowed on Marcus's pack and closed my eyes.

Without distractions, my new ability to sense the location of gargoyles pushed to the forefront of my awareness. They registered in my mind as unique bundles of energy, Celeste larger, based on her proximity, and Oliver smaller and distant as he circled in the sky. More faintly still were the six gargoyles inside the mountain behind me.

I could locate the baetyl with my eyes closed.

The thought pulled me from the edge of sleep. With this new power, I could detect *any* baetyl if I was close enough. I might not be able to get through its defenses, but I would be able to point right to it. It was the kind of knowledge people like Walter would kill for.

But no one would ever know. It would be my secret.

I woke at the abandoned Hidden Cache train station. The solid weight of Oliver pressed against my left side from my head to my feet, and his sunrise-orange eyes glowing less than a foot from my face were the first things I saw. I smiled and reached for him, groaning when the movement set off my body's litany of complaints. Oliver pressed his face into my palm and closed his eyes in contentment. The sun had passed its zenith, and Celeste didn't slow as she crossed the tracks, trotting across the quiet meadow on a narrow trail cut through the weeds by giant cerberi feet.

"Where are we going?" I asked, sitting up.

Marcus hadn't moved from his seat at the front of the sled, and the dark hollows under his eyes told me he hadn't gotten any rest, either.

"To see a man about a sled," he said.

The thought of seeing Gus's face when we showed up on his doorstep made me grin. "He's going to be outraged that we're not dead."

Marcus scoffed with feigned indignation. "As if something as feeble as Reaper's Ridge could kill us."

He couldn't hide his pained grimace when he shifted, but that didn't stop him from closing the distance between us and brushing a kiss across my lips. My heart sped in my chest, and I leaned into him, savoring the contact.

"Um, I'm going to fly around a bit," Oliver said, launching from the back of the sled. He dipped toward the earth, caught himself, and flapped upward into a long, lazy circle around us.

"We really should be headed toward a healer," I said.

"We are. Gus lives in a town with a small FPD base. It's how I was able to hire him on such short notice. Anyway, bases always have a healer on staff."

"Okay, healer, then Gus."

"Gus first. I'm not giving the scrawny bastard a chance to slip away."

"Good point. How much farther?"

"If Celeste can keep this pace up, another three or four hours."

I winced in sympathy. It would be faster than returning to Terra Haven, even if we had a train waiting to pick us up at the abandoned station, but it was still a long time for him to suffer.

"Do we have any greenthread left?" I asked.

I took Marcus's grunt as a yes and rummaged through his pack, retrieving a depressingly small roll of lamb's ear leaves and a mostly empty bottle of greenthread.

"Turn around so I can lift your shirt," I ordered.

He obliged and bunched his shirt into his armpits. The strips of previously gray cloth holding the lamb's ear bandages to his back were now blackened with dried blood and caked with a crusty green substance that alarmed me until I realized it was greenthread, not infection. I had to soak the bandages before I could remove them; then I dabbed on the last of the greenthread and layered the lamb's ear leaves over his flayed back.

While I worked, Celeste loped across mile after mile. Oliver returned to the sled every time he saw something he deemed amazing—a field of bright orange poppies, a dairy farm, a flock of caladrii—and I vowed to take him on a vacation so he could see more of the world than Terra Haven. I envisioned trips that included Marcus, our combined magic keeping Oliver healthy even in the most remote locations. Plus, the thought of having Marcus all to myself, without either of us in crisis or injured, sounded divine.

I wasn't surprised when Marcus nodded off, his head pillowed on the driver's seat, greenthread numbing what had to be the excruciating pain of his wounds. I stayed next to him, ready to catch him if he tipped toward his back in his sleep, and I watched the rounded foothills flow past and the weed-clogged trail grow into a slender dirt road, content to turn my brain off for a while.

My gaze returned frequently to Reaper's Ridge, its white peak prominent despite the increasing distance between us.

I couldn't decide which amazed me more: its quiet, storm-free expanse or the fact that I had not only climbed the ridge and survived, but I also could claim half the credit for disbanding all the deadly storms. The presence of the hidden baetyl ensured the ridge still wasn't safe for humans, but with its protective measures functioning correctly again, now people would be turned aside instead of killed.

Marcus jerked awake at sunset, making a quick assessment of the sled, the hills, me, and everything in between before relaxing again. Then he kissed me long and hard so I "wouldn't forget."

"Forget what?" I asked breathlessly.

"Me. You forgot me after Focal Park—"

"I did not!"

"And I don't want that to happen again, so . . ."

His second kiss lasted longer than the first, and I was almost disappointed when we reached the outskirts of a town a few minutes later. Nestled in a narrow valley and flanked by a patchwork of vineyards, it appeared far too picturesque to house Gus in its midst, though Marcus assured me we were in the right place.

Oliver returned to the sled, landing gracefully on the driver's seat. He bunched his body to fit on the narrow bench, and coils of his tail spilled to the floor, the red-orange carnelian gleaming in the final rays of the setting sun. By the time Celeste marched us through downtown, twilight had settled over the sleepy streets, but the sight of a gargoyle pulling a sled that appeared to be driven by another gargoyle drew people out to the walkways and windows to gawk as we passed. Marcus and I got as many curious stares, most likely because we looked like avalanche victims, recently freed from the rubble.

Marcus pointed out the Federal Pentagon Defense base

tucked behind the main street. Its high adobe walls and towers peppered with arrow slits loomed over the graceful architecture of the rest of the town, hearkening to a more dangerous era. So long as it included a healer and a working shower, I didn't care how militant it looked.

"Are you sure—" I started to ask, attuned to Marcus's growing stiffness as the last of the greenthread's numbness wore off.

"Gus first," he growled.

"Gus first," Oliver echoed, but his attempt at sounding menacing came out musical.

Marcus directed Celeste to a tiny, secluded cottage, where climbing roses coated the whitewashed siding, and pink and white blooms cascaded from the shingle roof to the diamond-pane windows. It even had a white picket fence wrapping the flower-filled front yard. I'd pictured Gus living in a rotting lean-to, most likely next to a stream that served as his drinking water, lavatory, and once-a-month bathwater. Or better yet, in a cave, where he slept piled atop his cerberi.

"Are you sure this is it?" I asked.

As if in response to my question, a chorus of howls emanated from behind the cottage, the harmony of three throats unmistakably a cerberus's. More howls joined the first only to be cut off abruptly at a sharp whistle.

"This is the place," Marcus said. He jumped down, and the tightening of his jaw was the only indication he gave that the movement hurt his back.

I wasn't half as graceful or prideful. My body had stiffened at every joint, and I groaned my way to the ground, clutching the side of the sled as I worked blood back into my feet and convinced my thighs they needed to support me. Beneath my shirt, dried greenthread and lamb's ear leaves crunched, and brown and green dust sifted from my cuffs and untucked hem. I ran a hand through my hair, futilely attempting to comb out the snarls, and settled for tucking dirt-coated strawberry-blond chunks behind my ears. I started to pat the dust off my pants but froze when I heard Gus's voice.

"Damn idiot woman had that FPD fella twisted around her pinkie finger. Not that I blame him; she was a looker, but no piece of tail is worth risking your hide on Reaper's Ridge." His voice floated around the side of the house, and I straightened, expecting to see him saunter into sight. His next words were inaudible, but his cackle set my teeth on edge. When a few other men joined him, I realized Gus must be entertaining out back.

"I disagree," Marcus whispered. "You're exactly the kind of piece of tail that's worth risking Reaper's Ridge for."

I snorted and rolled my eyes.

Oliver hopped from the seat, using his wings to glide to a silent landing. Even full grown, he wouldn't reach half Celeste's height, but his short stature didn't preclude him from looking fierce when he bristled his orange ruff and stiffened every spike along his spine. Gus's house should have gone up in flames from the heat of his glare alone.

Celeste's indignation had nothing to do with Gus's insulting conversation and everything to do with having been witnessed in her debasing role as a pack animal by half the town. The moment we stopped, she yanked free of the rope and stalked away from the sled, tail lashing. I followed her on hobbling steps.

"Thank you, Celeste. It would have taken us days to reach here without your help," I said.

She trained her hard amethyst eyes on me, nodding fractionally. Twelve hours of almost nonstop running against the loose rope had chafed a raw line into the onyx and amethyst feathers across her chest, and I healed the wounds with her consent. Despite her stiff posture, exhaustion weighted her body. After I assured her we would be fine without her assistance, she flapped heavily toward the FPD base, her black and purple body disappearing against the darkening sky.

We left the sled and circled the house, guided by the ambient light of the rising moon and the flicker of flames around the corner. Oliver loped at my side, wings tight to his body but his expression baleful enough to remind me of the apparitional gargoyles inside the baetyl.

"So here's this city twit with a fool notion of taming the ridge with a bunch of dud gargoyles," Gus continued, oblivious to our approach. "All of them were frozen stiff, and you couldn't lift a pitcher of water with the boost they gave off, but that wasn't going to stop her."

"No one ever accused anyone out of Terra Haven of having two thoughts to rub together to keep warm," a different male voice chimed in.

"They ain't got any money sense, either, praise the gods," Gus said with a chuckle. "Between delivering them to the ridge and what I'll earn when I pick up their corpses, I'll be building a new kennel before winter. Bless those poor, dead idiots."

The rumble of masculine laughter swelled. I almost felt like joining in when we rounded the corner and Gus caught sight of us. He choked on an inhalation and clutched his chest through a wracking coughing fit, never taking his round eyes off us. Or rather, never taking his eyes off *me*.

Oliver glowed in the firelight like liquid flame reshaped into an enraged dragon, and he hissed at Gus with undisguised animosity. On my other side, Marcus loomed, looking every inch the FPD warrior and equally as irate as Oliver. Without taking another step, he filled the empty space of the tiny patio and seemed to crowd the three men sitting around a small terra-cotta fire pit. Next to him, I should have been invisible, but Gus stared at me with the fixated disbelief of a man seeing a ghost.

The two other men jerked straight in their chairs. Both rivaled Gus in age, though the years had been kinder to them. Unlike Gus, they sized up my companions first, and the larger fellow's hand fell away from the heavy dagger at his waist when he met Marcus's hard eyes.

"Friends of yours, Gus?" the skinnier man asked. He clamped a cigar between his teeth and leaned back in contrived nonchalance, his eyes flicking back and forth between Oliver and Marcus.

"We're just three corpses come back to collect our due," Marcus said. He spoke softly, which only tightened the tension in the other men.

Gus finally looked at Marcus, and his breathing calmed to a wheeze. Shaking his head, he grabbed a glass bottle near his foot and took a swig of its amber contents. "You've got nothing to collect here."

"We had a deal."

Gus's companions flinched at the ice in Marcus's tone, but Gus waved his words aside. "You said you'd return the sled *after* you went up Reaper's Ridge. Yet here you are—"

"Yes, here we are," I said, stepping forward to draw Gus's attention back to me. My movement played the firelight across the shimmery amethyst scars on the backs of my hands, and the skinny man's mouth dropped open, freeing his cigar to roll down his chest to his lap. He stared, unaware, for several seconds before leaping to his feet with a curse and patting down the smoldering front of his pants.

Gus's face had lost some color, but he continued gamely. "So you have some sense after all, girl. How far up Reaper's did you get before you turned tail?"

"To the top. I really don't know what all the fuss was about. After we dispersed the storms, it was a pleasant hike and a great view."

"Dispersed the storms," he scoffed, but his gaze shifted to look over my shoulder toward Reaper's Ridge.

Up until yesterday, even from this distance, the wild flares of firestorms and sporadic lightning would have been visible on a clear night like this. Tonight, only the faint outlines of the dark hills against the starry sky defined the mountains, Reaper's Ridge just one among many shadowy peaks.

"Well, I'll be . . ." said the heavyset man, standing and squinting in disbelief.

"That's impossible," Gus said.

"Maybe for people around here, but not for a girl from Terra Haven." I couldn't resist the taunt. "Now, I believe you owe us some money."

Gus glowered at me, and I could practically see the gears turning behind his cagey eyes. He stood, spat to the side, and clapped his stained brown cowboy hat to his head. "I'll need to inspect that sled. If it's damaged..."

Marcus arched a brow and escorted Gus to the sled. I remained near the fire, enjoying the warmth almost as much as the discomfort of the two men who couldn't decide if they should stare at my face or my scars.

"How?" the skinny one worked himself up to ask.

"Gargoyles. Never underestimate them."

They both turned disbelieving eyes on Oliver. He yawned, displaying sharp incisors, and flared his wings so the light danced across them. If the men weren't impressed, they were fools.

"Fine," Gus said as he returned with Marcus. "I'll give you your money back."

"You'll pay us the full amount you promised," Marcus said.

"Do I look like I have that kind of money lying around?" Gus gestured to his threadbare clothing.

"You'll find it. Otherwise, I'll have a word with the captain of the base, and you can kiss any future contracts with the FPD good-bye."

Gus sucked on his teeth and glared at Marcus. "Fine. Wait here." He spun and headed away from the house up a shallow rise toward a long, low barn.

"You have a tendency of running away," I said. "Why don't I keep you company so you don't lose your way?"

Gus shot me a nasty glance over his shoulder, but his eyes were a little too wide and ruined his glare. When Marcus gestured for Oliver to accompany me, the young gargoyle leapt to the edge of the fire pit and launched over the heads of the two men in a spectacular display of agility and intimidation. The men cursed and ducked, and the skinny one fell out of his chair. Smothering my laughter, I strode after Gus, stretching my legs to catch up without running. For whatever reason, I made Gus nervous now, and I didn't want to ruin it by giggling.

The riot of barks set off by Oliver's landing confirmed the barn was actually a large-scale kennel, the kind where the individual cages were as large as horse stalls to fit the pony-size cerberi. The concussive *woof*s and higher-pitched baying rattled my brain in my skull once we were inside the enclosed confines of the barn, and I hunched against the deafening assault. Gus marched up the central aisle, mouthing inaudible curses but doing nothing to quiet the racket. Seeing my discomfort, Oliver loosed a sharp whistle and every cerberus in the building quieted between one breath and the next.

Gus spun and stared at me. I pretended not to notice.

"Thank you, Oliver."

"You're welcome," he said, oblivious to Gus's reaction as he loped along the cage fronts, touching noses with the cerberi as he passed.

Gus clicked his mouth shut and stuffed his hat tighter to his head. Heavy breathing sounds replaced the silence as dozens of panting muzzles pressed to the slatted fronts of the cages, all sniffing and straining to get closer to us. Fumes of dog breath did nothing for the already musty air, and I took shallow breaths, hoping Gus would be quick.

The wiry man stomped to the largest cage at the end of the barn, waiting until I was almost at his side before throwing open the door. Three enormous heads burst out of the enclosure, growling in unison, teeth chattering a soft warning. With a height that dwarfed the other cerberi, this one wouldn't have to stretch to crush my throat in any one of its immense jaws.

Gus checked my reaction, clearly expecting me to cower in fear. I crossed my arms and affected a bored expression, though if Oliver hadn't been beside me, his magical enhancement at the ready, I would have been shaking in my boots. Pretending I wasn't mentally preparing a dense quartz shield to protect Oliver and myself if the cerberus attacked, I raised an eyebrow at Gus in a fair imitation of exasperation.

"Your oversized dog isn't going to scare me, Gus. I survived Reaper's Ridge."

"So you say," he muttered. He barked a one-word

command, and the enormous cerberus sat. Two heads continued to glower at me, but the third turned to lick a slimy trail from Gus's collarbone to his hat. Gus shoved past the head with a grunt, crossing the kennel to unearth a small box from a niche in the floor. The cerberus tracked him with one head, the other two locked on me.

"You don't believe me?" I asked, studying the back of my hands. In the soft overhead lights, the amethyst scars appeared to shift of their own accord. I flexed my fingers, remembering how right it had felt to use the baetyl's power to grow crystal from my thin bones. I hadn't admitted it to Marcus, or even to myself until that moment, but I found the scars beautiful.

The cerberus leaned a head close to sniff me, and I extended my hand, forgetting to be afraid. Moist nostrils pressed to the scars, and a soft *woof* escaped a different throat. When I met the cerberus's gaze, he whined and lay down, resting all three heads on the floor in front of him. Eyes unfocused, I stared at the cerberus and stretched my shoulders, missing my wings . . .

Gus turned around with a glare, but his steps faltered at whatever he saw in my expression. I blinked, coming fully back to the moment. The memory of the baetyl faded, and I stifled a yawn. This time my lack of trepidation was unfeigned when I reached over the subdued cerberus for Gus's wad of cash. Gus hesitated, then smacked the bundle into my palm. He started toward the door of the kennel, but I didn't move out of his way as I counted the bills.

"This is only as much as Marcus paid you. The deal was half again as much for returning the sled."

"It was in full working order when I gave it to you—"

"Which is exactly how we're returning it, but you're right; I didn't factor in how much Marcus should charge you for repairing it. He's an FPD fire elemental, and everyone knows they get a good salary, so if we estimate his hourly rate . . ."

"Now hang on, there, girl. That's not what I meant."

"But you have a point. So why don't you hand over the *full* sum you said you'd pay to get the sled back, plus half of the fee you charged me to take us to Reaper's Ridge—seeing as how you got us only halfway there—and we'll call it even."

Gus's jaw muscle worked as his gaze flicked between my bland expression and the scars on my hands; then he spun on a heel to dig through his stash of money again. Oliver undulated up to the cerberus and scratched him behind one of his ears. I stepped back when the three-headed dog tried to get his back foot up to help Oliver out.

When Gus caught sight of his formerly intimidating cerberus practically rolling belly up for my gargoyle, his mouth pinched so tight I thought he'd crack a tooth. He slapped another stack of bills into my hand, and I took my time counting them, watching Oliver out of the corner of my eye and trying not to smile.

When I was satisfied Gus hadn't stiffed us, I stuffed the bills into my back pocket, wincing when I hit bruised flesh, and signaled Oliver that it was time to leave. He reluctantly loped toward the exit.

"Useless mutt," Gus growled. The cerberus stood and licked Gus's face affectionately before he could close the kennel door. A chorus of whines and pants followed us out of the barn.

Marcus's gaze sought mine the moment we emerged from the barn, his thunderous scowl softening marginally at the sight of us. Gus's friends didn't seem to notice the change in him, and they fidgeted nervously as we approached.

"I might have to go check out the ridge—see if you're telling the truth about the storms being gone," Gus mused as we stepped back into the firelight.

"Go ahead. But to shut down those storms, the gargoyles and I had to set powerful protection wards. You won't get close to the top—or to those mine shafts, if that's what you're thinking."

Gus had the grace to look embarrassed that I'd seen through him so easily. "If *you* got up there, I don't think I'll have a problem," he grumbled.

"Knock yourself out trying," I said. Memory of the pulsing migraine and menacing presence of the baetyl pursuing us stole the flippancy from my tone, making the words come out hard. I thought I'd ruined my exit, but Gus's troubled expression said otherwise.

We paused at the sled to collect our packs, and I handed the cash over to Marcus, expecting him to pocket it. Instead, he counted out what he'd paid Gus for the sled, then gave the rest of the money back to me. "You earned it."

I stuffed it into my bag with a soft sigh of relief. I would be able to pay rent and have some left over, maybe enough to replace the clothes I'd ruined on this trip.

I shouldered my bag and Marcus picked his up with one hand, letting it dangle rather than slinging it across his injured back. He reached his free hand out to me, and we twined our fingers together. Oliver squeezed between us, bumping our hands with his head. His jaw cracked in a tongue-lolling yawn, and he tilted against me. Marcus caught us both when I staggered under the gargoyle's weight.

"Do you mind if I fly ahead? I'm tired."

"Go for it. We'll be right behind you," I said.

He trundled a few steps forward, then flapped heavily into the air.

Marcus and I followed, walking hand in hand down the moonlit street, and I couldn't help thinking it would have been a lot more romantic if we both weren't injured and covered in dried sweat, pungent ointment, and half a mountain of dirt. I lifted my shirt and sniffed, grimacing. A bath couldn't come soon enough.

"Hang on." Marcus jerked to a halt, his expression comically troubled. "Did this trip count as a first date?"

I cocked my head, ruminating out loud. "We did stay overnight in a very exotic location. You even made me dinner. Yeah, I think that counts as a date."

"Well, crap. How can I possible top *that*?"

"You'll think of something." I stood on my tiptoes and kissed him, rejoicing in the realization that our adventures together were only just beginning.

Read on for an exciting excerpt from

A FISTFUL OF EVIL

the first in the international bestselling
Madison Fox urban fantasy series by
Rebecca Chastain

AVAILABLE NOW!

Madison's new job would be perfect,
if not for all the creatures trying to
eat her soul…

A FISTFUL OF EVIL

The interview was a catastrophe. It started out fine—better than fine. Kyle, the sales manager for the bumper sticker company Illumination Studios met me in the warm confines of a nearby Starbucks, purchased me a grande green tea, and selected a table in the corner, away from the door and the cold blast of November air every customer brought in with them. Soft music, cappuccino-machine clacks and whirs, and the murmur of conversation created a cocoon of privacy.

I handed Kyle a copy of my résumé, determined to prove myself to be the mandatory employee for the boring junior sales associate position. I wasn't particularly qualified and I would normally have rather peeled hangnails than perform cold calls—which is what I strongly suspected the position entailed—but four weeks of unemployment, seven failed interviews, and escalating credit card bills proved very strong motivators.

Strong enough for me to ignore the desperate reason I'd applied for the job. *Never trust your soul-sight,* I told myself for the thousandth time. But my imminent eviction trumped mistrust of my bizarre, mutant vision.

Kyle dropped my résumé to the table without glancing at it. He scrutinized me over the top of his dry cappuccino. Kyle exuded salesman, from his maroon button-up shirt and khaki trousers to his thinning brown hair with its frosted tips. His face was pinched, as if someone had pressed his baby flesh between their hands and pulled, extending his nose and pulling his lips and eyes in tight. He couldn't have been much older than me, despite the sullen brackets around his mouth and deep grooves between his eyebrows. Maybe his expression fell into disapproving lines naturally.

"How many years' experience do you have, Madison?" Kyle asked.

"Specifically in the bumper sticker business, none, but I believe my time at Catchall Advertising will—"

"I don't care about the bumper sticker crap. I care about your experience in the field."

My weirdo radar, dulled by the overpowering mix of desperation and determination, flickered to life now.

"I honed my sales skills while working as a saleswoman at Sundage Cars. My experience there taught me how to connect with people from all walks of life." Though it hadn't taught me how to sell a car. In the six months of my employment as a used-car saleswoman, I sold a grand total of zero cars, which is why David Sundage, my cousin-in-law and owner of Sundage Cars, had fired me at the beginning of September. But I wasn't going to concern Kyle with that minor detail.

Kyle set his cappuccino down on the table and leaned back in his chair. "How old are you?" he asked.

"I'm not sure I understand the relevance—"

"What regions have you worked in before this?"

Regions? "I've worked mainly in Roseville since I—"

"With who? Not with Brad or Isabel." Kyle leaned forward, his dark eyes intense.

Who? I eased my tea to the table and ran my palms down the sides of my black knee-length skirt, telling myself it was only nerves that were making Kyle seem so volatile.

"Um, most recently with David Sundage," I said.

"Where are his headquarters?"

Headquarters? What is this, the FBI? Hadn't he bothered to read my résumé?

"Down Douglas," I answered, pointing vaguely west toward Douglas Boulevard and the car lot.

"Before that?"

"Also in Roseville, at Catchall—"

"Look, we can both stop playing this game. I don't care about what jobs you've had to take between IE positions." Kyle deflated into his chair with a gusty sigh. "To be honest, you're the only qualified person to apply for the job—my job. I've been ready to transfer for months now, so I'm not going to make this interview hard on you. I want you to take this job as much as you want it. I just need to make this interview look good so Brad signs my walking papers, okay?"

I nodded and tried to look like I understood more than the English words he used. I didn't know what he meant by "IE positions," and I knew I wasn't qualified for his sales manager position. I wasn't even qualified to be a junior sales associate, but who was I to argue? Managers probably didn't have to make cold calls, which automatically made the job more appealing. Plus, a management position would pay better, and I was pretty sure I could fake it until I got caught up on my bills. By then, I could find a more suitable job. Something more Indiana Jones and less Bridget Jones.

"Okay, let me make this perfectly clear," Kyle continued. "Which wardens have you worked with?"

"Wardens?" As in prison?

Kyle leaned forward, placing his hands on the table. "What's the largest evil you've ever tackled? A wraith? A pissed-off dryad?"

I cast a quick glance around for a candid camera, noting the nearest exit in case I needed to make a run for it. I'd been nervous on interviews before, but never because of a mentally unstable interviewer. Was that why Kyle had insisted we meet away from the company office? Did he even work for Illumination Studios?

I eased my hand through the strap of my purse and slid it onto my shoulder, careful not to make any sudden movements that might spook the deranged man. "I don't think I'm the right person for the job, after all," I said, and pushed away from the table.

This is why I never used my soul-sight, never followed its false leads. I shouldn't have made an exception for this job. To the marrow of my bones, I knew soul-sight was untrustworthy.

"Hang on, Madison," Kyle said, grabbing my arm as I started to stand. I froze. "You're definitely the right person for the job. You're the first enforcer to walk through that door in nearly two weeks."

"I don't even know what that means. I'm going to save us both some time and leave now." I tugged to free my arm.

"Holy crap! You're a rogue." Kyle jerked away from me, shaking his hand like I'd given him cooties. Unbalanced, I fell back into my chair.

"That explains your age," Kyle said, speaking more to himself than me. "And your job history. You haven't been playing games with me—you really don't know . . ."

I stood again as he trailed off, and his gaze snapped to focus on my face. "It was nice to meet you," I said by rote. "Good luck with—"

"One question." Kyle stood, cutting off my escape. He towered over my five-foot-ten frame by a good eight inches. Despite his wiry build, the odds weren't in my favor that I could knock him down before he could grab me.

Taking a deep breath, and reminding myself that I was in a safe public place filled with people, I said, "Okay. One more."

"Did you apply because you thought you could pretend to be qualified for a sales position or because the ad glowed?"

My breath caught. The fact that the job description in the "Help Wanted" section had glowed in soul-sight had been an inexplicable anomaly. Dead, mashed pulp couldn't glow. It wasn't alive. It didn't have a soul. But hearing that Kyle knew about the glow set my arm hairs on end. No one knew about soul-sight except my best friend, and that was only because I'd told her. Soul-sight was my own personal aberration.

Seeing my hesitation, Kyle plowed on.

"Three decades as a rogue has got to be a new record. I'm not sure why you chose to come out of hiding, but I'm not letting you get away now, not when I'm this close"—he pinched his forefinger and thumb together—"to escaping this puny region for some real action."

"I haven't been hiding. I think you're mistaken—"

"Come on. We both know you're not qualified for a sales position even if it did exist," Kyle said, flicking my résumé. The crisp white paper skittered off the table to the floor. "But if you could see the glow, you *are* qualified to be an enforcer. Hmm, let's see, how to explain this to a thirty-year-old rogue?"

"I'm twenty-five," I corrected softly, wondering why I was still standing there, why I hadn't stepped around Kyle and walked out the door.

"You have the ability to see the world differently than this 'real world,' right? Black and white? Plants and animals glow all pretty and clean. People look like they're wearing snowy-weather camouflage. Is this ringing any bells?"

There was definitely a ringing in my ears. He'd just described soul-sight. My knees wobbled and I sank disjointedly into my chair.

Kyle sat across from me, shaking his head with amazement. "I can't believe you've maintained a rogue status for so long. I mean, I understand the appeal of not having a boss, but you're also not on anyone's payroll. Why not become a real enforcer and get paid for it?"

Paid to use soul-sight? Has he infected me with his insanity?

"I, um—"

"Trust me, this region's not hard at all. It's a good place to cut your teeth, but it gets monotonous real fast. Still, let's see what you've got. Tell me what you see here."

"A coffee shop," I said, not quite willing to believe he and I were talking about the same thing.

"Fine. I'll go first." He twitched his long, pointy nose and grinned at me. "You've got great color. Very pure. Which is how I knew you were an enforcer. No *atrum* in sight."

I shifted in my chair, irrationally pulling my suit jacket tighter to cover myself, but Kyle had already turned away.

"Now, that guy behind the counter, he's not the honest type. Look at the way *atrum* coats his fingertips and wrists. Disgusting."

Kyle grinned at me. I tried to remember to breathe. He

was truly talking about soul-sight. I wasn't the only person with the ability. All brain activity got jammed up between that thought and his statement that people—*he*—got paid to use soul-sight. Once I could formulate a complete thought, I was going to have a lot of questions.

"Go ahead, look around in Primordium. I'm going to see if I can attract us a little fun," Kyle said.

For the first time in ten years, I intentionally blinked in public.

I gripped the edges of the table for support against the wave of dizziness that broadsided me whenever I switched between visions; then I purposely examined my surroundings. The coffee shop was slate gray, all color nonexistent in this vision. From the floor (which I knew was tiled white) to the wooden tables to the chrome espresso machine, every inanimate object was shades of charcoal. The overhead lighting didn't exist in soul-sight—*in Primordium,* I corrected myself. Shadows didn't exist in Primordium, either, not traditional light-created shadows. Something worked in this vision to give depth to objects, but trying to focus on it was a recipe for a migraine. The only bright spots in the room were the people.

I forced myself to examine the man behind the cash register to verify Kyle's description, fighting against soul-sight-avoidance instincts honed over the last ten years. My fingers tightened on the table. The barista's fingertips and wrists were smeared black, like he'd had a run-in with a dirty chimney. The rest of his arms were pale gray, as was his face. I knew from experience, those dark patches represented some immoral choices and actions. Light gray was normal for a human; black was pure evil. Only animals and plants were pure white in Primordium. The barista's smudged wrists meant he'd made some bad choices, but I couldn't tell what. That was only one of the flaws of soul-sight.

The only person's soul I'd ever seen that was as pure as an animal's was my own. Since I was far from perfect, I figured I couldn't see my own flaws. That was fine by me. Seeing my soul felt like looking inside myself, and it was a sure way to induce stomach-churning vertigo.

I swiveled my head to look at my companion, fully expecting him to look like a variation of every other human I'd ever seen.

Kyle, the plain-looking salesman, glowed brighter than most searchlights. I lifted my hand to shield my eyes, but it was as impractical as shining a flashlight in my eyes to shield them from the brightness of the sun.

"Aha! There are a few curious imps. Figured there would be with the traffic in here," Kyle said. He was too bright to see his facial features, almost too bright to see a solid outline. When he talked, I couldn't tell if his lips moved. It was one of the creepiest things I'd ever seen.

I had a thousand questions for this man—why had we never met before? Why did he refer to me as a rogue? Could he please dim himself?—but what came out was, "A curious what?"

"Imp." His glowing head swiveled toward me. "You have killed evil creatures before, right?"

I shook my head. "What evil creatures?"

"Amazing. Truly amazing. It's like you've been hiding under a rock, invisible to both sides." He shook his head in wonder. "You've not imploded a single imp? Not even a small one?"

"Maybe I have," I said, belatedly offended and not sure why. "What do they look like?"

Kyle laughed loud enough to draw several stares. "No

shit. A rogue with zero experience." He chuckled again. "The best Brad can attract to his puny region is an untrained nobody with no clue. I'd love to see his face when—" He raised his hand to forestall my next question. "Never mind. You've got the ability; you're trainable. Brad won't turn you away, not when he's so desperate for an IE. Ah, that stands for *illuminant enforcer*, which is the job I'm leaving to you. So let me give you your first demonstration of what a true enforcer does. Watch carefully."

I tore my eyes from his shining aura. There was no after-image like with real light, which was a good thing, because I'd have been blind for a half hour after staring so hard. Logic said the bright light of Kyle should have cast shadows all over the room, but in this strange sight, logic didn't apply.

I wasn't sure where I was supposed to look, so I scanned other customers.

The coffee shop was busy but not full, with groups of two and three people scattered around the free-floating tables—mostly college students or businesspeople escaping the office. People firmly rooted in reality, not looking at dirty souls and talking about illumi-something enforcers and Primordium.

I focused on the group of four people to my right. Like everyone else in the room, they had gray dollops peeking through the V-necks of their shirts and flecks of black soot defiling their hands and wrists. I could see their features faintly through their bodies' natural light, and I flushed with embarrassment when all four turned to stare back at me. I rarely let myself use my soul-sight around people; despite my discomfort, it was heady to use it so blatantly now. Of course, to them it just looked like I was staring rudely.

"Do you see the imps?"

I swiveled back to Kyle and blinked against his brightness. Unobtrusively, I leaned against the table while the world spun back into color.

"They're the smallest of the evil creatures, little blobs of pure evil. Hardly enough brain matter to function. Just enough to recognize food and attack it."

Not good. This is so *not good.* I wished I were back at home with my cat, Mr. Bond, and a good book or a TV show. Something ordinary. I did not want to be talking with the only other known person with soul-sight who kept insisting there were evil creatures visible to only us. I felt like a character in a horror movie right before they slowly turn around and come face-to-face with a monster. Seeing evil on people's souls was bad enough. I didn't want to see—let alone come into contact with—something purely evil.

And yet, how could I *not* look?

I blinked, carefully focusing away from Kyle first.

I scanned the room again. Baristas. Customers. Books and CDs. Coffee bags. "What am I looking for?" Kyle didn't answer me. Movement under the nearest table caught my attention. An inky black chinchilla-like blob sat on the table's base, its glowing eyes watching me.

"What the hell is that?" Anything with life was always a version of white. Even the sullied souls of the sadistic still glowed with light undertones. Nothing living was all black —it was life that made everything glow. Furthermore, animals were never tainted by ambiguous moral choices like humans; animals were *always* white. The tiny fluff ball of blackness was darker than the inanimate objects around it. It was black—solid black. Impossibly black. Either there were varying degrees of life I'd never encountered and this was the zombie equivalent of life, or this creature—this pile of dust with bright eyes—was pure evil.

"Madison, meet your first imps," Kyle said.

The imp cocked its head at me, clearly curious. Curious meant it could think. Curious meant it was trying to puzzle me out. A thinking *evil* creature was interested in me. Abandoning my job hunt and moving back in with my parents suddenly seemed like a great idea.

The imp hopped toward me.

I lurched to my feet, sending my chair careening into the people behind me. Scrambling around the table, I put distance between myself and the creature. Its eyes tracked me. It hopped out from under the table until it was less than two feet away from me. I tensed to flee.

Kyle waved his radiant hand in front of the imp the way a matador waves a cape for a bull. Like a bull, the imp charged. I squealed. The imp disappeared.

He'd said imps, *right? With an* s*?* I spun around, looking for more.

I spied three behind Kyle's chair. Like the first one, the dark creatures were fixated on him. In a group they lunged. I jumped back, tripping over a chair. Windmilling my arms, I fought for balance while trying to keep the evil creatures in my sight, but gravity won. In a cacophony of wood and metal and flesh, I crashed to the floor. When I looked back at Kyle, the imps were gone.

"Miss? Are you okay?"

Reality popped like my ears had just unplugged. I blinked. The world swam. I rolled to my side. From my position on the gritty floor, I could see a circle of black-clad feet, and more approaching. Baristas. Everyone in the coffee shop had gone deafeningly quiet, making the cheerful jazz sound like it was blaring. I realized three things simultaneously: (1) *everyone*—from the patrons to the dishwasher—was staring at me; (2) I must look like I had gone absolutely, start-raving mad; and (3) my skirt was hiked up to my hips. *Shit. Can you die from embarrassment? Please?*

I untangled myself from the rungs of the chair I'd tripped over; stood faster than I should have, assisted by the adrenaline of embarrassment; and yanked my skirt down so that it covered me to my knees. I patted at my hair, pulling a bit of muffin out of a clump and wiping my hand on a napkin. And I assured everyone that I was fine, convincing no one.

How could I be fine? I'd just learned that I wasn't the only person with soul-sight—or the ability to see in Primordium. Worse, there were evil creatures that lived alongside us, visible only in Primordium. Creatures that gazed upon me and Kyle with the same loving look I reserved for triple chocolate fudge cake. Somehow Kyle had made them disappear, but for all I could tell, it was magic, because how did you use a sight to make something vanish? I wouldn't have believed it if I hadn't just seen it. It was the equivalent of a person using their normal sight to move an object; it just didn't happen.

Only it had.

ABOUT THE AUTHOR

REBECCA CHASTAIN is a feminist, animal advocate, and nature devotee. She believes empathy is a hero's trait and love is a motive, an inside job, and a transformative energy that shapes each person's world. She is the *USA Today* best-selling author of the Gargoyle Guardian Chronicles, the Terra Haven Chronicles, and the Madison Fox urban fantasy series, among other works.

If given the opportunity, Rebecca will befriend your cat.

Visit RebeccaChastain.com
for free stories, bonus materials, updates, and so much
more!

– NOW AVAILABLE –

Don't miss a one-of-a-kind hilarious adventure from *USA Today* bestselling author

Rebecca Chastain

TINY GLITCHES

Dealing with her electricity-killing curse makes living in modern-day Los Angeles complicated for Eva—and that was before she was blackmailed into hiding a stolen baby elephant and on the run with Hudson, a sexy electrical engineer she just met.

"I laughed out loud too many times to count."
                                        –Pure Textuality

RebeccaChastain.com

9 780999 238530